Messenger

VIRGINIA
FRANCES
SCHWARTZ

Holiday House / New York

This historical novel is based on the lives of the author's mother and grandmother.

The author would like to acknowledge the following people for their participation in the writing of this book:
My mother, Frances Tyios, whose voice gently guided my pen; my uncle, Phillip Chopp, true keeper of our family's stories, for his endless patience and enthusiasm in the telling of them; my editor, Mary Cash, with her ever amazing ability to see clear into the heart of the story; Edie Rubin, principal extraordinaire, for understanding; my Long Island writers' group, who encouraged the telling of my grandmother's stories; my brother, Sinclair Tyios, for remembering; my Friday lunch group, for their gift of friendship; and always, forever, for my husband, Neil, keeper of the houses.

The extracts from William Wordsworth's poems on pages iv, 221, 222, 277 are from William Wordsworth, *The Complete Poetical Works* (London: Macmillan and Co., 1888).

The translation of the psalms on pages 1, 79, 141 are from the author's family Bible, *The Holy Bible*, Douay-Challoner Text with Psalms and New Testament written in the Confraternity Text (Chicago: The Catholic Press, 1950). Readers may note that the psalms in this book are numbered differently than in many versions of the Bible. The Douay-Challoner translations and versions based on it use a slightly different numbering system for the psalms. Both numbering systems are cited here, with the Douay-Challoner first and more familiar in parentheses.

The prayer on page 104 is one the author remembers from her childhood.

The extract from Leigh Hunt's poem "Abou Ben Adhem" on pages 179–180 is from *The Oxford Companion to English Literature*, ed. Margaret Drabble (Oxford: Oxford University Press, 1995).

Library of Congress Cataloging-in-Publication Data
Schwartz, Virginia Frances.
Messenger / Virginia Frances Schwartz.—1st ed.
p. cm.
Summary: Based on the lives of the author's mother and grandmother,
tells the story of a widowed Croatian immigrant trying to keep
her family together in the mining towns of Ontario in the 1920s and 1930s.
ISBN 0-8234-1716-6
[1. Silver mines and mining—Fiction. 2. Family life—Ontario—Fiction.
3. Single-parent families—Fiction. 4. Croats—Canada—Fiction.
5. Ontario—History—20th Century—Fiction. 6. Canada—History—
20th Century—Fiction] I. Title.
PZ7.S4114 Me 2002
[Fic]—dc21 2002017108

For my grandmother
forever shining
in my memory

Frances Brozovich Chopp Stampfl

1898–1996

The music in my heart I bore,
Long after it was heard no more.

—Wordsworth, *The Solitary Reaper*

Contents

Schumacher, Northern Ontario 79

Hamilton, Southern Ontario 141

Messenger:
One who comes with something to tell

Messenger

In the beginning
he was a touch.
A light brush.
Air
against my dark skin.

Above me
in the shadows.
Hidden in the corners
of the hushed cabin.

Watching.

A voice
in the middle of the night.
Frances!
A call to awaken
like he had once called me.

Then he was everywhere.

In May blossoms,
summer wind
blowing across the wheat field,
and waves tossing
on the lake's blue face.

If only we listened.

Cobalt,
Northern Ontario

Even though I walk in the dark valley,
I fear no evil;
For you are at my side.

—Psalm 22 (23)

Chapter 1
The Visit
October 12, 1923

After Pa left for his job in the mines that October morning, Ma had a sign.

Hundreds of crows darkened the skies as they flew right over our cabin. They circled it around and around. Quartering, it's called, when they gather like that. When Ma heard their cries, she ran to the window. She was a tiny woman, not even five feet tall, but her back was straight and her walk quick. I can see her looking up, her heart pumping quicker than their wings, her hands on her belly to soothe me. I was unborn, hidden inside the bulge at my mother's waistline, pushing her gingham dress out like a barrel.

"Don't worry, little one." She must have whispered to me, so that my brothers, still asleep, wouldn't hear her. "Everything will be fine."

But Ma believed birds gave omens. An omen stops you in your tracks. It's as if a shadow passes over you and marks your future. All that day, my mother shivered and piled on sweaters, building the fire high. That afternoon, when the sun blazed on the maple leaves so that the hills looked red with flame, she finally let my brothers out to play.

At first, Ma did not see the two men marching down the road. She stood in the dried field of buckwheat, between the dirt road and the log cabin Pa had built, watching my two brothers chase each other in and out of the waving stalks. Phillip so tall at six, thin and dark, swift as wind. William waddling behind him at two, plump and flushed.

Her eyes were on her children. She watched them like a hawk does its newborn, her bright blue eyes darting every which way for predators. We lived in the middle of the bush, as she called it. Pa had moved us a year before to this acre of land, a mile away from town where the silver mines were. The evergreens reached so high, they blotted out the sky. Wolves, bears and foxes prowled everywhere.

It was when my mother pulled William up from the ground that she turned and saw the men. From a distance, she could tell they were miners, for they still wore their tin hard hats as if they had left the mines suddenly. Their hands were empty of pickax and lunch pail, yet their arms hung heavily at their sides. They kept a slow and steady pace down the road, straight toward her.

Ma stiffened. Phillip saw the flat look on her face, how her teeth were set in one tight line he had never seen before. He grabbed William by the collar as he squirmed away from Ma, yanking him to a stop. All three stood frozen, looking down the road.

The miners paused a few feet away from them. Both men took off their hard hats. They kept their eyes down. One of them cleared his throat.

"Are you the wife of Phillip Chopp?" he asked. "The office said we'd find you living back in these pine woods."

Ma reached out with one hand for my brother's shoulder and another for the buckwheat that bent in her grasp, bracing herself against their thin weight.

"Ma'am, there's been an accident down in the mines this morning. One of the shafts caved in. There was no warning. Ten men were trapped. Not one was saved."

The men looked up then, up at the sky.

Ma kept her eyes drilled on the two men, as if trying to hold them in their place before they said another word.

But they kept on.

"We came to tell you your husband passed away in the mines before we could reach him. Miners will carry his body home soon. Our wives will come to lay him out. Sorry to bring you such news, ma'am."

It was so still that my brother could hear the wind passing through the stalks of buckwheat, shaking their little heads. The cry startled him like a train whistle at his back, shrill and warning everything to get out of its way. It was Ma screaming.

My mother went straight down to the earth, Phillip said. She clawed the ground, digging through plant roots, through clay, until she scraped her fingers against hard gray slate.

The earth was a drum, he said, that our mother beat upon.

Chapter 2
The Anointing
October 12–13, 1923

Ma must have fainted in the field, for the two men carried her into the cabin. She was light, though her body was swollen thick with the weight of me. A pale woman with a bun of coppery hair, undone now, falling loose like a wild animal's mane. The men stepped carefully along the path, as if they held glass. My brothers followed without a sound.

The cabin soon filled with Croatian women from the mining tenements, a cluster of about a hundred cabins at the base of the mines. The miners' wives were scrawny women, their dark hair hidden by bandannas, their heavy woolen skirts swishing across the floor. Only a few spoke English. They tiptoed in one by one, whispering in Croatian, holding tight to one another's sleeves. Some tended our mother in her big iron bed. A woman carried William away, his arms and legs kicking. His cry cut the air, razor sharp. She hurried my brothers into the back bedroom and closed the door. In the late afternoon, she gathered the curtains, drawing darkness into the room, telling them to go to sleep.

It was only when Aunt Tracey, Ma's sister, came from

town that William finally stopped crying. He let her press a cup of warm milk to his lips, whisper stories in his ear and rock him until his eyes shut. When she thought both of my brothers were asleep, my aunt shut the door and left them. But Phillip bounced back up, flattening his eye to the slat of wood in the door. In the big room, the women drifted, bringing a hush into our home. My brother's milk, untouched, turned ice cold.

At dusk, wagon wheels rolled to a halt outside. Ma wailed like a lost animal. The women moved back from the door. Uncle Matt and three miners carried our father inside and laid him out flat on two pine planks set on top of a cedar chest. An old woman stripped him of his miner's clothes, black with soot and soaked in blood. She washed his body down. In a tin bucket, she dipped a cloth over and over, turning the water black.

Ma watched from her bed, a rag over her forehead, her body stiff as a tree. Her eyes followed the woman's hands as she worked, drying and dusting Pa with white powder, then dressing him, lifting his arms and legs into his shiny black wedding suit. Finally the old woman folded Pa's hands across his chest and wound a rosary of black beads through his fingers.

"Leave the rest to me," said Ma in a voice thin as vapor.

My mother struggled to get out of her blankets. Aunt Tracey stepped beside her.

"Sit up slowly, Frances. You've had quite a shock."

Ma sat up, shut her eyes and would have fallen back had not our aunt righted her again.

7

"There, now. Give yourself time."

The women held my mother by each elbow and guided her across the room. They sat her in a straight-backed chair beside Pa. Ma reached for a brush then and stroked Pa's thick chestnut hair until it gleamed.

Two candles were lit on each side of his body. Pa lay like he was sleeping but his chest did not move. There was such a stillness around him, it reminded Phillip of the time a summer windstorm blew in and just before it did, it was strangely quiet. Even the birds stopped singing.

Everything paused to listen now, suspended.

The miners' wives surrounded Pa in a circle, standing watch all that night. When someone died, you had to guard the dead one's soul, lest the devil steal it away. All around the room, white sheets covered the mirrors like ghosts, hiding our faces from death. At any moment, death, hovering close by, might see our reflections and grab us too. My brother did not dare step into that room. So he watched too, from behind the door. Sleep kept coming to him though. He struggled to open his eyes again and again, hoping to see our father awaken.

As he drifted off, Phillip heard Ma mumbling as she fingered Pa's rosary beads entwined between both her and Pa's hands. Her lips moved but her eyes stared into the distance as if she were no longer in the room.

Early the next morning, my brothers awoke to a rap on the door. They stepped out into the big room. The Croatian women had vanished. Only Aunt Tracey and Uncle Matt had stayed overnight. A man dressed in black stepped into the cabin with a shiny black book in his hand. It was old Father Gorman, stooped over and half blind, the only Catholic priest in Cobalt. His skin was pale as a potato against all that black, as if he lived underground. He walked over to the cedar chest. Ma was still sitting there, beside Pa, rocking herself back and forth.

The priest set his hand on our mother's shoulder. She rose up, held her arm against the wall to steady herself and sank down to her knees.

"He suffers no more, Frances. He was a strong man, a good husband and father. He is with God now."

Father Gorman bent over Pa. He placed the Bible on top of his chest and a crucifix near his head. Everyone knelt. Our aunt folded my brothers into her long skirts. The priest chanted words deep and low, sounds Phillip had not heard before, in a language he did not know. The priest anointed Pa's forehead and chest with oil, touching him in the shape of a cross. Then he blessed my father with holy water, dripping it over his body like tears.

"In nomini Patri et Filio et Spiritui Sancto."

After the anointing, Aunt Tracey picked my brothers up so that they could look down at Pa. Paleness sealed him like wax, making him look unreal. His lips were slightly open, as if his last words hung there, secrets he never told. Afterward, my aunt led Ma back to bed and pressed a cloth over her eyes to block out the light. My two brothers stood at the foot of the iron bed and watched our mother toss and turn and fling the covers away like she was drowning.

I was inside, floating, listening, my ear pressed to the thick chambers of flesh separating us. The world was close by but I could not reach it. My mother's heart beat like a fist, banging *why, why, why*. I heard my brothers' weeping as they kept watch. Ma was far away and Pa had not awakened, as they had hoped he would. He lay, unmoving, for three days and nights in that cabin, his eyes shut by the miners, his body anointed with holy water.

For that time, no one has words. Those days were like whispers.

The world had come to a stop.

Chapter 3
Baby

October 19, 1923

They buried Pa in a cemetery just outside of Cobalt alongside the other nine miners. They piled the dirt up high in a round heap, one stone at his head, another at his feet, to mark the spot. Snow was on its way, the miners warned, but come spring they would plant a slate tombstone in the ground. The frost would just heave it up if they set it down now. A long line of Croatian, French and Italian mourners, miners and their families, paraded into our cabin, day and night, afterward. They brought funeral pies of salty meat and potatoes baked in a pastry shell, smoked sausage and sweetbreads.

But Ma wouldn't eat any of it. She sat, limp, in her black mourning dress, leaning her head against the wall. Her belly tightened with sharp pain. Later she said she was sunk too deep in grief to notice the cramps taking her breath away, then the letting go. Not until the pangs tore through her without stop, driving her back to bed with water gushing to the floor, did she know she was in labor with me.

"The baby's coming too early," Aunt Tracey murmured, counting the contractions. "She's not due for a month yet."

It kept up for two days. Uncle Matt brought the old midwife. She massaged Ma's belly, turning me around with firm hands to point the way out. Everyone waited outside on the porch, keeping watch again. Our uncle kept his head down. The miners' wives paced. My brothers hid behind some pines and overheard the women murmuring.

"Some say a baby's a blessing at such a time," one said. "She'll have to stop mourning to tend a baby."

"She's already got enough mouths to feed," muttered another.

"Pray the baby's all right. It's been a shock for the child too."

Their words spun around in Phillip's head until he felt ready to burst. As soon as the midwife opened the door to the cabin, he bolted inside to study Ma himself before the miners' wives had a chance to come in.

"It's just birthing, child." My aunt noticed his pale face. "Done it myself twice. Probably do it again too."

"Don't worry, son," coaxed Uncle Matt. "The Brozovich family is strong. Emigrated from Croatia to Calumet, Michigan. Farmed all their lives. Your ma and aunt were brave enough to leave Calumet with your pa and me to take a chance on the mining boom here. She'll bring this baby in fine."

Phillip refused to be comforted. My brothers both stood watch and waited. In the high iron bed, Ma writhed, squeezing the bedposts, covered in sweat.

That night, I was born, a week to the day after my

father died. I arrived early, barely eight months. I had to come. Ma needed me. The old midwife whose hands first touched me, pulling me from darkness into light, was the same woman who had laid my father out.

"She's come to tell you your husband is in heaven," the midwife told her. "She must have brushed against him coming into heaven when she left it."

They say I hardly made a sound. I was born into the hush of death and dared not disturb it. I was tiny and dark-skinned with a weak cry. My hair and eyes were coal black, darker than either of my parents'. My brother said I had big eyes that ate up everything. Ma used to stare at me lying so still in her arms, my huge eyes studying her back.

My eyes were mirrors of my soul.

For my first months, most everyone shook their heads around me, wondering if I would live. Ma tucked me inside her shawl, keeping me warm and safe.

"That little one won't live the week out," a miner's wife worried.

But my family had hopes for me.

"What will you call your new daughter?" Uncle Matt asked Ma.

He was a big man but he was quiet and gentle. His waist was as wide as a woodstove and he loved to eat just about everything.

"You were hoping for a girl this time." Aunt Tracey smiled. "After two healthy boys, you finally got your little girl."

Our aunt was the opposite of Ma. She was big-chested, wide-hipped and always laughing. Folks joked her voice could travel a mile.

But my mother just sighed. "I never thought of a name. Phillip said he had a name all picked out but he wouldn't tell me until the baby was born."

"Must have been your name, Frances," decided my aunt. "She's the firstborn girl. She should be named after you, like you named your firstborn son after your husband."

My mother looked down at me. "Frances you will be, then. But I'll always call you Baby. You're my last child. All I have left of your pa."

Chapter 4
Adrift

Fall 1923

Ma hardly left her bed for months. A flat look had settled on her face. Something stole the light from her eyes. She didn't smile anymore. She hardly said a word. She grew thinner and thinner, stumbling as she walked. That fall, she dragged herself between the cookstove and the bed, holding on to the wall.

Aunt Tracey stayed with us at times. She cooked and cleaned our cabin. But she always had to leave again to tend her own children, our cousins, five-year-old Helen and eight-year-old Paul. She also cooked meals for the Cobalt miners who were bachelors. By the end of the shift, come seven o'clock, dinner for fifteen had to be set on her table. She was always rushing in and out of our cabin, Phillip said, her skirts flying like wings behind her.

Croatian miners chopped our wood and heaped it up for the long winter ahead. They killed a whole pig, smoked it and hung it to dry in the barn. They covered over our root cellar before deep frost hit so that no wild animal would dig up our beets and potatoes. They also tended our animals. They'd ride in on horseback, long after dark, the clumping of their horses' hooves breaking the silence of the bush.

Come December, when the snow blocked the road, making our aunt's trip too long, we were alone in the cabin for the first time. Ma drifted off after she nursed me. She couldn't seem to get enough sleep. She hungered after it all that winter.

So my brothers had to tend me. To William, I was a toy or a pet. I must have slipped through his hands once or twice, for Phillip wouldn't let him hold me for long. Phillip took charge of me. He thought I would die like Pa, I suppose. He smothered me in woolen blankets so that I filled out round and plump, though I was skinny as a stick.

He remembers standing with me in his arms in front of the window, watching the snow fall in a thick blanket of hush all around us. Once it snowed, it stayed, one layer on top of another so that by deep winter, the snow was piled as high as the house.

"Just like in Calumet," Ma whispered, her eyes flat and gray.

The days were endless white. Phillip dug a little tunnel between the door and the woodpile and another path out to the chicken coop and barn. My brothers took turns pulling each other in a sled back and forth over those paths. The weight of them barely pushed down a flake of that snow. It was the kind of snow you could walk across and never sink into. The crunch of your footsteps traveled for miles around. You could even hear your own breath, my brothers said, echoing in your ears.

The nights outlasted the days. When darkness fell, my brothers sat by the stove with me in a wooden cradle, for long hours. They took turns rocking me. I lay on my back, swaying back and forth. In those moments between wakefulness and before sleep came, I watched the ceiling. So high above my head, the wooden beams set by my father's hands, and the hidden corners where shadows danced in the firelight. The darkness held firm, as if it paused to look down at me. As if there were strings between the shadows and me, swaying my rocker long after my brothers grew weary. Then my eyes finally shut. And the shadows wrapped around me, warm and tight, pulling me into dreams.

I think Ma saw it too. She didn't say a word about it then. I often caught her looking up, as if someone called her name, her chin lifted to the sky, just like mine, her eyes so dark, all the blue gone out of them. Wondering what was there. Her face seemed to pull in all the light around her. Then she'd sigh and shake her head and go back to whatever it was she was doing.

The days grew colder and shorter. The air was always clouded by snow squalls. Nights, a hush settled around us. Wind pushed at the door. Wolves howled on the hill. But inside that cabin, no one spoke. Perhaps a log shifted in the woodstove and that was all. No one visited once winter set in for good. The miners scurried in the darkness to tend our horse, pigs and chickens, always hurrying, for after sunset, the temperature dipped far below zero with each passing hour. They headed back to town without disturbing Ma.

She lay still in bed. Sometimes, my brother said, she watched the door for hours after dinner like she used to, waiting for Pa to come home from the mines. Listening for the thump of his work boots on the porch.

Ma was far away that first winter. We had to wait for her to come back to us.

My brother paced restlessly, watching our mother. He wanted to shake her back to life but didn't dare say anything to her. He never mentioned one word about Pa either, although I am sure he wanted to. His memory of Ma is of her wrapped in sheets, not hearing anyone, but mostly closing her eyes, drifting long hours. To my older brother, my mother was a china vase, fragile, cracked down the middle. He thought she might make the wrong move and break in two, leaving us on our own. But Phillip saw Ma only from the outside.

I didn't see her like that.

When I was a baby, I felt I was still inside, holding on to that invisible thread that had bound her and me together. When Phillip carried me over to her for nursing, I lay my head against her chest, breathing in and out the same breath. It was where I longed to be, hearing that sound I had known for eight months, her lungs pushing me up and down like a seesaw. I closed my eyes and drifted, back and back, to a time when I was inside and Pa was close by and Ma was smiling and the world was round and promising.

I knew from the start, from no sign in the outside world, that Ma would go on.

I am the one who was sent. My father's messenger. He who could no longer stay, sent me instead. For his was the voice that told me early to go to her.

To awaken her.

My need will be so sharp, my hunger so engulfing, that I will call her out of the darkness she has stumbled into.

She will know me by my cry.

Chapter 5
The Stranger
Winter 1923

Uncle Matt brought a stranger to our cabin that December. My brother knew right away that he was a gentleman when he heard him coming. He stamped the snow off his heels and left his boots outside before he knocked. No miner would do that. When he entered, he took one look at Ma, sunk in bed like an animal in its winter den with a baby at her breast, and he took off his hat.

"Come in," invited Aunt Tracey. "We've been expecting you."

"This here is the manager of the mining office," Uncle Matt told Ma.

Our aunt helped my mother sit up in bed. Her eyes were blank as she stared at the stranger. She did not speak. She squeezed me tightly to her nightgown as if she was afraid the stranger would take me away.

"I've come to discuss the contract, Mrs. Chopp. When a family's had a loss such as yours, we provide for them. First, there's an allowance for your children. Come spring, there'll also be a settlement."

My mother had no voice to answer him, but our aunt did.

"How much?" she asked in a sharp tone.

The stranger counted us one by one.

"For three children, it'll be thirty dollars a month. Ten dollars a child. That's your widow's allowance."

All Phillip heard was one word. Widow. A hard word, like an insult slamming against the walls.

"For how long will she get the allowance?" Uncle Matt asked.

"For as long as she is a widow."

Our aunt and uncle let out a deep sigh. The cupboards were almost bare.

"Come spring, you say"—my uncle cleared his throat—"there'll be a settlement too?"

"A thousand dollars," the manager replied. "So this family can start up again."

All this time, Ma had not acknowledged the man. She kept her eyes down, watching me instead.

The manager cleared his throat and fiddled with his hat. "Ma'am, I must speak up." He stared at her. "I would be remiss if I did not tell you to leave this place. Without your husband, it will be hard for you and the children to live out here on your own."

My mother's eyes shifted his way then, noticing him for the first time. Then she looked outside at the tall pines standing straight up like guards against the bluer-than-blue sky. She turned her head as if she were listening to the creek that had trickled nearby so that in summers, it filled the house with its voice all night long. My brothers knew at once she was thinking of Pa.

"New miners move here all the time. We could rent

your cabin to them. We'd be willing to help sell it too," he offered before he left. "But leave as soon as you can get on your feet."

Aunt Tracey said nothing, but she had nodded when the man spoke and looked at my uncle. They both seemed to sit up taller after the man's visit, as if he had lightened their load.

Afterward, Ma and I lay apart from everyone in the big bed, rocking back and forth. But Ma traveled away from us all, farther than I could reach, perhaps all the way back to a sunlit day in Cobalt when Pa last smiled at her by the evergreens.

But the stranger had come to remind her. To name things. To define her. His words ate up the air we breathed.

Leave now, widow, echoed in my brother's head.

There was no place to go. Cobalt was all we knew. It was our home. There was nowhere to go without a father.

A Letter from the Old Country

December 19, 1923

One day in December, Uncle Matt brought the mail from town. Ma always received letters. That was the only way families far away from each other could keep in touch. There were no phones in any of the miners' homes. One letter had traveled all the way from Severin, Croatia, Pa's hometown. It was from Pa's sister Rose, postmarked October 1, 1923.

My uncle and Ma both shook their heads, that the mail should take so long, especially at a time like this. Aunt Tracey had written to our aunt Rose over a month ago about Pa's accident. We had not heard from her since.

"It was written before your husband passed away," said Uncle Matt.

Ma's hands trembled as she opened it. She sank into her chair.

October 1, 1923

Dear Brother and Wife,

I am writing this to you urgently. There is something I must warn you about. You may think it some superstition from the old country. You may not want to listen. But I have to tell you. I've had a dream. I can't get it out of my mind. I dreamed of broken shoes on the ground. The men around here who work in the mines told me such a dream is an omen of death. I know of no one who works in the mines in our family except you, my brother. I beg you not to go to work once you receive this letter. Promise me that you will not go. Promise me, Frances, that you will not let him go.

Your loving sister,
Rose

I can see Ma sitting there with that letter in her hand and my aunt Rose in Croatia with Ma's letter in her hand, an ocean between them. I see them both look up darkly, holding the death letters, their mouths bitter, downturned.

The warning came too late. Pa was not saved.

Chapter 6
Coming Home
Christmas 1923

Ma did not even know it was Christmas that year. She had forgotten all about presents.

"Spend Christmas with us," Aunt Tracey coaxed her. "You shouldn't be alone at a time like this. For the children's sake, stay with family."

My uncle came on Christmas Eve to get us. Ma changed out of her nightgown for the first time since Pa's burial. She put on her best dress, the one she wore only at funerals. She dressed in black from hat to boot. Even her eyes looked dark. Uncle Matt tied our wooden sled to our horse Charley and my whole family piled on, one behind the other: Ma in back, holding us in; Phillip in the front, leaning into the bends.

It was a crystal clear night without a moon, but there were a million stars to help us see our way. Charley's shoes clumped heavily against the frozen ground. Steam puffs from his mouth spread like clouds of fog around us. Ma clutched the rail of the sled and stared straight ahead, her mouth grim and flat.

Our aunt and uncle lived in the tenements surrounding the mine. Long, narrow, dark, one-room log houses.

There were beds along the walls with a cookstove in the middle and only one window in front. But Phillip thought it wonderful. Helen and Paul ran around, laughing and flushed, anticipating our visit, and Aunt Tracey had baked butter cookies and roasted turkey the whole night long, filling the cabin with warmth and delicious smells.

We stayed up late for midnight mass. In the bare unheated church, filled with echoes of our movements, Father Gorman read the names of those who lived with the Lord. Our father's name, Phillip Chopp, was pronounced out loud in that packed church along with the names of the other nine who had died with him that day. It was like a bell calling us, spilling sorrow tears down our cold cheeks onto our winter coats. When we left the church, Ma lit a remembrance candle for Pa. It lit up the darkness, wavering, leaping for air, straight up to God.

On Christmas Day, my cousin Paul played with my brothers, spilling out the door onto the icy wooden walkways. They ran to see the twenty-foot-high Christmas tree set in the center of the town. Lumberjacks had chopped it down on the mountaintop and dragged it there. The miners had decorated it with tinsel and shining paper and set a white angel on top. Snow adorned its limbs as if it still stood in the forest, Phillip said.

But Ma stayed inside, holding me on her lap with Helen close by, studying me, the three of us in a tight circle. Helen stroked my cheek, fascinated by my smallness and my softness, like a doll that was alive. Ma kept silent and apart, eating little, while Aunt Tracey fussed around the stove. In her forest green dress, my brothers said, Aunt Tracey looked as sparkling bright as that Christmas tree.

Everyone ate their fill that night. Turkey. Roasted potatoes. Stuffing. Thick, greasy gravy. Tart cranberry sauce. Bread pudding. After dinner, all the children received presents from our aunt and uncle. Our uncle had carved and painted wooden trains for the three boys. They zoomed around the cabin, yanking rows of trains behind them, yelling at the top of their lungs. Helen wore the new woolen cap and mittens that her mother had knit. Aunt Tracey gave me a Raggedy Ann doll that she'd made from bits and pieces of cloth Ma had saved. She was sewn out of a burlap sack that had stored potatoes. Her overalls were cut from Pa's jeans, and her eyes were buttons from Uncle Matt's jacket. Sitting on my mother's lap with me, the doll seemed like one of the family, her black eyes watching us.

Early the next morning, we awoke to clanging and banging. The whole cabin rattled. Even the iron bed we lay upon shifted and squeaked on its legs. My brothers lifted their sleepy heads from their pillows.

"Don't be frightened, children!" our aunt called out to us. "These cabins are set right above the mining shafts. The men have gone back to work this morning after the holiday. They're drilling a hundred feet below us."

Ma sighed. "That's why your pa moved out of these tenements to the bush. Wanted us to have peace and quiet."

The mining shafts descended straight down, Phillip said, beneath that town. All the tenements sat on top, never still, except on Sundays and holidays, their floors shaking and walls rumbling. My brothers wanted to see the mines and there was no stopping them. Paul led them down the street to the mining pit, just a block away. It was a big hole in the ground where the miners descended each morning and disappeared, searching for silver. Where our pa had gone down too, and had to be carried out.

Drifts stretched out sideways in long tunnels like greedy fingers leading out from the shafts. Some led a long mile out. Iron buckets, filled to the brim with silver chunks, were hauled up to the street all day long. But the miners remained hidden underground. Eleven hours a day. Six days a week. Nine dollars wages a day.

"It was like a black hole with no bottom," Phillip whispered to me. "A cave. You wouldn't catch me going down there."

That night, Uncle Matt drove us back to the cabin in the bush, Charley dragging our sled. My brothers huddled in their scarves and pulled their caps down low over their faces, but there was no hiding from the cold. The stars were dimmed and the air damp, smelling of snow. The north wind stole everyone's breath away. Up ahead, the cabin was dark. Icicles circled it, hanging like sharp knives from the rooftop. Nobody waited for us, keeping the fire lit. Ma paused on the porch, unwilling to enter.

Inside, the cold had moved in, stiffening the bedsheets. Water left in buckets had turned to ice. Uncle Matt stoked the stove while my family huddled and paced in their coats. Ma boiled water for tea and we slowly began to thaw.

But as soon as Uncle Matt fed the animals and left for town, Ma plopped down into a chair, her body rigid. Her face turned gray, as if she had no life left in her. Silence moved into the spaces around us. The night, so vast and empty, closed in. The three of us children so small, alone in that cabin, with our mother, thin and tight, in her black dress . . . it was only then that she cried, slamming her fists on the table, her sobs rising, building higher and higher like flames. So high pitched, they seemed to crack open the night.

If I close my eyes and try to remember, this is what I see: Outside, the night creatures pause in their journey. A doe turns her head our way, her liquid eyes deep and brown. An owl lands on the pines, soundless and alert. All the animals listen in the cold black night.

Chapter 7
In the Middle of the Night
Winter 1924

That February, a blizzard arrived, bringing days and days of snow. It piled up three feet overnight and just kept falling. The temperature dipped to minus forty. Wind howled and snow drifted in gusts, slamming at the cabin walls, pushing to get in. Nobody in Cobalt could get out.

We were snowbound.

One dead cold night, my brother awoke in pitch blackness, shivering in the big iron bed where Ma had moved us all to keep warm. His breath made smoke clouds in the frozen air. Ice was thick on the inside of the windows where Jack Frost had crept in. No fire burned in the stove. William, beside him, was bundled up asleep in the blankets. But Ma and I were both gone.

He heard an ax slam down outside, shaking the cabin. *Whack! Whack!* In the next moment, Ma stumbled through the doorway with an armload of wood. She kicked the door shut behind her and threw the wood down by the stove. It was only then that Phillip saw my tiny head peeking out of Ma's jacket, my body pressed flat to her bare skin.

Ma looked over at Phillip staring out of the covers.

"In a few minutes, I'll brew hot tea and you'll soon be toasty warm."

The fire had completely died out. My mother set kindling pieces down and began to coax the flame back to life, fanning it with her breath and stirring it up with a poker. She lit it over and over again, but each time the wind blasted down the chimney and blew it out. Finally she held a torch of burning paper up the chimney and the kindling lit up. When the fire blazed, she ran outside again. She carried back scoops of snow in her bare hands and piled it into the kettle.

Only then did she crawl into bed beside my brothers. She rubbed their numb hands and feet hard. Soon her warmth surrounded them beneath the covers. The stove cooked away. The kettle steamed. Phillip said we were like a sandwich, with William and me pressed in the middle and him and Ma on the outside, holding the heat in. My mother put sips of hot tea to all our lips. Everyone drifted off to sleep again.

Later that morning when Phillip awoke, Ma was busy at the stove, clanging and banging, building up a roaring fire. The ice inside the windows had melted. Sunlight shone through the glass. The dark, cold night seemed like a dream.

"Good that you're up, my babies. I'm making breakfast."

She stirred up cornmeal and snow until it thickened into polenta. Steam blew all over the cabin in clouds from the kettle. Then Ma called my two brothers to get out of bed. The only thing left in the pantry was black tea that the adults sometimes drank instead of coffee. She made them drink it now, pouring lots of snow into the kettle with just a sprinkle of tea leaves. They sipped it without sugar, for there was none.

After breakfast, Ma turned to my brothers. Though her hair was loose and wild, a light shone in her face, softening the sharp angles of her cheekbones.

"I've been grieving so, I forgot time altogether. I thought I was gone just like your pa. But, in the middle of the night, I heard someone call, '*Frances!*' Clear and loud. It was your pa warning me to get up. The baby was ice cold."

"Was Pa really here with us?" Phillip looked around the cabin.

"He came to help, son. When he saw me get up, he moved on."

She set her hand on my oldest brother's shoulder.

"Phillip, you are the man in the family now. You must be the one to wake me if you see me sleeping. I can't let the fire go out again. Will you promise to do that, son?"

Phillip had never dared to awaken Ma. In her big bed sleeping, she was far away. But that day, he had to promise her to do it.

"No one's checked the animals all week," she worried. "The miners won't be coming in this weather. The poor creatures must be starving."

They went to the barn to check on Charley, the pigs with their three young babies and the flock of chickens. The rotting smell of manure and musty straw hit their noses right away. The barn had not been cleaned since fall. The animals were thin and weary and watched them with sharp eyes. Charley bent his head, sifting through a few twigs of straw, searching for something to eat. But the rooster complained as usual and the hens skittered around. The animals were all alive, though unkempt. Together, Ma and Phillip raked the floor of the barn, heaping up a pile of manure and soiled straw.

"It will make a good garden come spring," Ma told Phillip.

It was the first time she had spoken about the future. To my brother, there were only endless winter days without Pa. Time had stood still since the cave-in.

Phillip climbed up to the loft and threw down a fresh bale of hay and filled the troughs with food. Ma brought in snow. The heat of the animals would soon melt it into water, she said. They left potato peelings for the pigs and gathered eggs in their pockets. When they left, the hens were clucking away happily. Phillip smiled, too, for that night, they would eat an omelet for dinner.

That day, Phillip became the man in our family. His work had begun. He was seven years old.

Chapter 8
The Package
March 1924

Ma spent evenings after the dishes were washed and the other chores done sitting by the table in the glow of a kerosene lamp. My brothers were tucked under their covers and I was asleep in my rocker. Phillip said she sat up close to the lamp and read through all her old letters. She squinted in the lamplight, for it cast a haze on the pages. Her nose almost touched the words.

She did this whenever a letter came from the old country or Calumet. I picture her then, only twenty-five, with lovely copper hair the color of rusty pennies. I see it falling around her thin, sharp face in waves and curls that had fallen out of the bun she had fixed that morning. She hardly breathed as she read.

Sometimes there were letters from her sisters in Calumet, pleading with her to come back home. We could live on their parents' old farm with them, they said. There was plenty of room, even with Ma's two sisters, their husbands and kids. But my mother shook her head over those letters.

"I can't go back home," she decided. "If I go back, we'll be poor like the rest of Calumet all our life. There's nothing to do there but farm. The mines are dried up. The boom is over there."

Letters always came from Ma's oldest sister, Aunt Annie. She and Uncle Jack were the first ones in our family to emigrate from Calumet to Cobalt ten years before us. We had followed in their tracks. By the time I was born, Uncle Jack had saved enough money to buy his own place. They moved to a farm in southern Ontario, in a village called Simcoe. My aunt wrote to us about the flat land and the three cuttings of hay over the long hot summers. Ma sat back in her chair and always closed her eyes after she read Aunt Annie's letters, traveling far away to that warm place.

When she was done, she folded the letters back into their envelopes and tucked them in a shoe box under the bed. She blew out the lamp with one puff. On cold nights, she folded me deep inside her woolen shawl and crawled into bed, her mind filled with words I could not hear. All those voices probably ran around in her head: her five sisters still living in Michigan, Pa's sister in Croatia, and her cousin Joseph in Severin with his dreams of coming to America.

One March day, a package arrived from Calumet. It was from Ma's youngest sister, Aunt Elsie. Inside was a letter. Ma sat a long time reading and rereading that letter. Quiet tears washed down her cheeks. They didn't take over her whole body and set her to rocking like when Pa had just died. They seemed like remembering tears, sweet and soft as summer rain.

From inside the package, Ma drew out little brown

packs of seeds that rustled when she moved them. Our aunt had painted pictures on them. Phillip and William both peeked over Ma's shoulder as she fingered each pack, stroking them like she did my face in the evenings to set me to sleep.

"Leaf lettuce," she told them. "Soft as butter, these leaves are. Chive seeds. Once you plant them, they stay forever. They taste wonderful whipped into cottage cheese on a slice of bread. Now we'll have our own."

Ma looked out the window at the patch where the garden used to be. She was smiling for the first time that winter.

"Chives come early, boys. We'll be eating them before Easter."

William pulled out more packs of seeds.

"Peas!" he called out. They were his favorite vegetable.

"We'll plant them early with the lettuce and chives. They'll be on our plates by June."

There was more. Garlic bulbs, white skinned and dry. We wouldn't eat them now but would wait to press them into the soil come spring. Squash and tomato seeds were there too, for planting later in the summer garden.

My brother said Ma came back to life at the end of that winter. He swore it was the seeds that set her right again. Those vegetable seeds had been in our family for many generations. In 1888, aboard the boat sailing from Croatia to America, our grandparents had carried seeds carefully folded into handkerchiefs. The seeds came from plants that their own great-grandparents had planted generations before in Severin.

As Ma sat by the table that night, her hands shuffled through the seed packs as if they were a deck of cards that could change her luck. But it was Ma that Phillip studied. She was thin after that hard winter, her hair matted down and unwashed, her eyes circled darkly, but she was no longer still and lying down. She sat straight up. Her eyes, which had been flat and gray for months, looked clear blue again.

That night while Ma nursed me, Phillip spoke of Pa for the first time.

"I miss Pa," was all he said.

Ma had not talked about our father in the months since his leavetaking. Just that one morning after the fire had gone out in the middle of the night. But his name was everywhere in that cabin. In his wool coat, still hanging by the door. In his work boots, standing up straight, ready to be walked in. His name was frozen inside us all. Now his name had slipped out into the open where we all heard it.

Ma jerked her head up and stared at Phillip.

"Pa?" William piped up. "Is he coming back?"

"No, son." Ma looked out the window. "We won't see him anymore."

"Where did he go?" William begged.

Phillip cut him an elbow, but Ma's voice interrupted him.

"God took him. But sometimes, I feel him right here in this cabin, looking down, wondering and worrying what will happen to us. Like he's got one foot in heaven while the other's still with us."

She looked around the kerosene-lit room, dark in the

corners, black at the windows. The light held at her face, touching the angle of her pointy chin. The cabin was so quiet, they could hear an owl hoot from the pines.

"He comes when I need him most. Like that night he woke me. We might have frozen to death. Sometimes, he looks in to check on us. I try to show him how you boys and the baby are growing. But he still worries. For he always comes back."

"I wonder if he suffers anymore," said Phillip.

Ma shook her head. "He's a spirit without a body to tie him down. He lives with God now. But when he left, his pain was everywhere. He didn't want to die."

"Why did he leave us, then?"

"These last months, that's all I've asked myself. Why? That word has wrung me out. But I've come to believe God wanted him. God had plans for him and for us, too. We just don't know what they are."

"Perhaps Pa knows why," my brother wondered aloud.

Ma paused. "Each time he comes, I sense him a little lighter, a bit brighter. Like he's spinning into air. Turning more toward God and away from us. Listening to what God tells him. Accepting what happened."

"Do you miss him, Ma, like we do?" William finally asked.

"I thought I'd die without him. But now, as I work, I sense your pa all around me. Then I'm not so lonesome. As if he were still here, reminding me what to do. I remember wonderful things, too. Like how he studied the stars with Phillip on summer nights."

"He wasn't afraid out in the bush," Phillip remembered. "He loved it here."

On summer nights, Phillip told my younger brother, just before the new moon when the sky was darkest, he and Pa sat on tree stumps behind the cabin. There were more stars than sky. Millions of them freckled across the blackness. You could see smoke rings of your breath in the air.

Ma looked out the window and always called to them, "Best you come in now. It's getting late. Too damp for that child."

She never joined them. It wasn't the cold she was scared of. It was the wolves. They sang from the hills some nights in the winter and spring. You didn't hear them much in the summer, though. Perhaps they crept on silent paws, Ma worried, ready to pounce. She always made Pa take his gun with him just in case. Pa never thought of using it.

It was the stars he was after.

"Don't worry about those wolves," he called back to her. "They won't come close. Our smell is enough to keep them away."

Then he'd laugh and laugh at the stars, his head leaning back to look up at them. The air rang like bells with his laughter.

After Phillip told William the story about our father, he drifted off. Later that night, he awoke to the clunking of wood. Ma was stoking the stove, scattering sparks of light in the pitch blackness of the cabin. Her shadow shifted across the ceiling, a giant over them all. Phillip blinked, half awake, half asleep. Perhaps it was really Pa's shadow up there, he thought, hovering above them, watching and worrying as Ma had said. Pa was the one who had always awakened in the middle of the night to feed the stove. Not once had he let the fire go cold.

The night didn't seem so dark anymore. The longest nights of winter were behind them. Pa was still close by, Ma said. He was looking down from the stars.

Chapter 9
Planting Seeds
April 1924

Every single day that April, Ma picked up clumps of earth and squeezed them between her fingers to see if the ground was ready. If a clump took on the shape of a ball, it was too early to work the soil. Her precious seeds would rot. Only when the dirt fell between her fingers like sand was it ready. It took days to work the garden. Ma and my brother carted manure from the barn and raked it through the soil. Finally, Ma tucked her seeds in the ground.

I was wrapped in a blanket, the ends of it tied around Ma's neck, swinging back and forth on her chest like a monkey. She kept me there while she worked, for I was crawling everywhere by then: in the dirt, under the cabin, behind the bed. I wanted to touch everything. I could fit anywhere.

Ma could dig for hours, but Phillip was plumb tired of planting in no time. Dirt sifted inside his shirt and clung to his nails. He sat outside in the early spring sunshine, keeping an eye on William running around. The next day, both my brothers expected the plants to be there.

"Plants take their time," Ma explained. "They come up when they're ready."

The wind was raw enough to whip your face red. There were still snow flurries. Then a spring storm dumped six inches of snow on that garden. When it thawed, lime green sprouts poked up.

"This here's the lettuce," Ma pointed out. "It's so soft, it bends in the wind. Not like those peas, wiry as rope and twisting everywhere."

The garden was all Ma thought about. Each morning, she'd stick her head out the window to admire the plants as if they were babies she was tending. Around the garden, Pa had once strung a fence, half chicken wire, half wood, but Ma had made the garden bigger that year and most of it was unfenced. She planned to build one the first sunny day.

One bright morning, the earth seemed like it was just born. There was not a cloud in the sky. It was only April, but it felt like the world had come back to life after a long, sad winter. The stream was wild, gushing with snowmelt. Even in the cabin with the windows shut, you could hear its roar.

Ma decided it was a great day to go to town. The fence could wait. She tied Charley to the wagon, not sure what straps went where. Everyone changed into their good clothes. Ma set me in an egg basket, wrapped up snug in a blanket. For the first time in months, we rode together in the wagon—except the person at the reins was not Pa, gently clucking to the horse, knowing the exact way to turn. It was our mother, with her lips flat and her forehead wrinkled, her eyes looking dead ahead on that road rutted with mud. She was just going to go. That was Ma for you. Here and there as they rode into town, Phillip saw folks staring at us going by. In those days, women did not travel without their husbands.

Our first stop was the company depot.

"I'm Frances Chopp," Ma announced to the clerk behind the counter. "I've come to pick up my monthly food parcel."

The clerk looked up at the dark hat and coat she was wearing and the crocheted shawl around her shoulders, cloaking her in blackness. It set her apart. The clerk knew at once who she was. Ma was a widow, one of the women who came alone for their supplies. He checked behind the counter for a row of boxes. In that town lived families like us who had lost fathers and brothers and sons to the mines, leaving a black hole in their lives. Somewhere they too walked in black. Those families are like spiders clinging to a web, Phillip thought that day, trying to stay alive.

Phillip helped Ma carry the big parcel to the wagon. They didn't wait to get home to look inside but peeked right away. It was stuffed with cornmeal, flour, tins of sardines from Nova Scotia, preserves, smoked trout, bitter chocolate, sugar, coffee, cans of string beans, and a sack of potatoes. It seemed like Christmas with all that food.

"We'll save ten potatoes for planting," Ma said, smiling. "Come fall, we'll harvest our own. Big and smooth and creamy."

On the way back home, a wagon wheel got stuck in a rut in the road. The wagon sank down into the mud. Ma coaxed Charley ahead by yanking on his collar, but the harder she pulled, the deeper the wheel sank. We were hours on that road. Phillip went into the woods for logs to pry the wheel out. When that didn't work, Ma heaved her whole body against the wheel. Finally, the wagon creaked on.

The sun had set by that time, and a damp chill was coming up from the ground. My brothers' pants were soaked with mud. Inside the cabin, the stove had gone cold. Ma bustled about as if she were following orders from someone: filling the kettle, stirring the wood up, sprinkling cornmeal in a pot, slicing potatoes. We ate our meal in darkness and instantly fell asleep.

The next morning, Ma stomped outside in her heavy leather boots, shaking the cabin. She bent down to the garden and stroked her hand across it. All the plants had been chewed down to the ground. Only the chives were untouched. Ma's fists were squeezed tight.

"Where did the plants go?" William grabbed her skirt.

"I should have fixed that fence yesterday," she muttered.

"We could plant again," Phillip offered. "We still have seeds."

"Too late for peas." Ma sighed. "The lettuce will come back, though. Its roots are strong."

"Who did it?" William wondered.

"It's not a who. It's a what. It came in the night or early this morning. A rabbit or groundhog. Maybe a deer."

We'd see rabbits hop in the grass if we awoke so early that it was still misty out, but never a deer close to the house. A huge woodchuck had had babies behind the barn the year before.

"I'm going to keep an eye out." She frowned. "Leave it some bait."

Ma dropped a moldy carrot in the middle of the garden. The next morning, just before sunrise, a boom awoke Phillip. Ma's shotgun was aimed straight at the garden, the end of the barrel still smoking. A dead groundhog lay flat beside the carrot, its feet splayed out. Phillip didn't even know our mother knew how to use a gun. The truth was, she had never touched one before.

"That's the last time it'll come looking around here for something to eat," Ma told him. "It'll be our dinner instead. Today, we'll plant more seeds, then build a new fence. Nothing will ever get in again."

She took the bullets out of the gun and set it safely down.

"Get me a bucket, son, and a knife. A sharp one."

She sank to her knees and skinned the animal. All that day, she mended the fence and kept running inside to stir up groundhog stew with potatoes and spring greens from the woods. It was greasy and thick with flour and it sank into Phillip's stomach like lead, making him full in no time. William took one look at the brown shreds of meat and wouldn't touch it. But there was nothing else to eat. Ma wouldn't touch our supplies. They had to last all month. So William finished his bowl. It was meat folks all craved in that cold country. Only meat could keep them warm.

William remembered the warm polenta Ma served me with clumps of peach preserves that Aunt Elsie had sent from Calumet. I sat in a high chair, globs of peaches on my cheeks, waving my spoon in the air and laughing at everyone.

"You were the lucky one," he told me. "You didn't have to eat that groundhog."

At the Cemetery

June 1924

In June, we visited Pa.

The air was sweet with perfume. Purple clusters of blossoms like scrunched-up fists sprang up beside the grave. Uncle Matt had planted a lilac bush there, Pa's favorite flower.

Phillip doesn't remember much about it except for the tombstone. It was set in the ground, standing straight and thin like a feeble gray soldier, rounded off at the top. He couldn't read much then, but he could read the name. It startled him to see it carved there, for it was his own name staring back at him.

Phillip Chopp
Father. Husband.
1891–1923
Gone to God.

Tears ran down my brothers' cheeks and Ma started weeping loud and hard. That started me bawling. They kept passing me around from hand to hand, Phillip said, trying to calm me. Aunt Tracey paced, rocking me in her arms. But I wouldn't stop. I kept on. Not until we finally drove away did I quiet down.

They say babies don't know where they are. But I had visited my pa. Though I couldn't see him, I felt him all around us. He looked down at us, his tears falling heavily, joining ours.

Chapter 10
The Angel Came
Fall 1924

It was a year, and still the settlement hadn't come as the manager had promised. The mine had no extra money to give Ma. The manager asked her to wait. She had no choice. But she didn't sit still. She harvested the garden that fall. Onions, garlic, potatoes, beets, carrots and winter squash filled our root cellar. Enough to last all winter, Ma hoped.

On the first anniversary of Pa's death, Uncle Matt drove us out to the cemetery. My brothers laid dried wildflowers at the foot of Pa's tombstone. The adults stood a long while. Ma cried and so did our aunt. Helen carried me off with the boys, who were chasing one another in and out of the miners' tombstones. Those graves stretched in long lines across the field. Row after row of thin slate stuck out of the grass like crooked teeth.

It was then that Helen noticed all the angels engraved on the tombstones, holding flowers in their hands. Their wings, lifted behind them unfolding. Their eyes, stony and wide, watching us. The boys made a game of counting them. As soon as they saw one, another angel popped up like magic. Thirty-seven in all, Phillip boasted. They were all beautiful, of course, he said, with shoulder-length wavy hair and swirling long robes, looking out with kind faces at the mourners. They alone seemed to understand death. They were the only ones who could smile at death and see a blessing.

For dinner that evening, Ma roasted a rabbit she had shot, along with acorn squash and potatoes from our fall garden. Everyone settled by the fire afterward, watching the red flames through the open door of the woodstove. Phillip told Ma about all the angels they had seen that day. She had smiled to hear of them guarding the cemetery where Pa slept.

"Why are there so many of them there?" wondered Phillip. "They outnumber the flowers and the prayers carved on the stones."

"To remind us," answered Ma. "There's another world, like a veil, behind this one. Angels look so peaceful, you just have to trust death is not the end."

William interrupted, "What is an angel?"

"A spirit that lives with God. It comes and goes between God and earth to bring us messages. To help us."

"I can't believe they're real," he said.

"There's angels and devils both. Each is powerful. They both fight for our souls." She studied the shadowy corners of the cabin. "You can't see them, but you can feel them. They are everywhere."

"But how do you know for sure?" Phillip insisted.

Ma stared at him a good long time, as if looking through him.

"The angels visited me once. They didn't stay long, but it was enough to change everything. It made me believe in them."

My brothers begged Ma to tell the story. That night, after many months of silence, she told them something that had happened in Calumet when Phillip was three. She had already moved to Canada when she received a telegram to go back home. Her mother was dying. All eight sisters met in Michigan.

"When I saw my mother, I felt my heart was about to burst. She was like a candlestick burned down to the core," Ma began. "She slept most of the time. Sometimes she told us stories about the old country. But the pain stopped her. Then one day, her favorite cat died. It set a black shadow over us like an omen of death."

She paused to look at my brothers. Their eyes were stuck on hers.

"That night, it was my turn to stay awake with my mother. It was breathless hot. I bathed her in cool water and slipped outside to catch some fresh air. Something brushed my arm. It flew past me into her open window. The air turned bright and white. As soft as if feathers touched me."

Goose bumps broke out over Phillip's arm. He waited for Ma to continue.

"I ran inside. My mother's room glowed like it was freshly painted. She slept peacefully. Her pain had gone. At dawn, she woke us all up. She sat straight up in bed and pointed to the window. 'The light! So bright!' she called to us. 'Wings are filling the room. Do you see it?' My sisters all shook their heads. My mother looked straight into my eyes and spoke for the last time. 'The angels are here. I've been praying for them to come for me.'"

Ma's words lingered in the air, touching my brothers' skin, sinking down to their beating hearts.

"What happened then?" my big brother asked.

"She fell deeply asleep, into a coma. The world was silent that day. Not a breeze. Even the cicadas refused to sing. That evening, my mother opened her eyes and stared out the window. A breeze lifted the curtains. You should have seen her face. Delicate. Radiant. Like a bride. She was gone. Gone with the angels."

Then she told us how she opened all the windows in the house to let her mother's spirit fly out to God, just as our grandmother had taught her to do when someone died. That is what we long for, she had been told, to go back to God as a spirit, leaving our broken body behind. To be set free.

For a long while after the telling of the story, there was silence in our cabin. A log shifted in the stove, startling everyone.

"If the angels had not come for her, I could not have gone on. But the instant they came, her pain left. I knew I could accept her leaving me."

William was the one who asked, "Did the angels come for Pa, too?"

Ma turned to him with reddened eyes.

"Maybe they did, son, but I didn't feel it. I was too deep in mourning to notice anything. I kept calling your pa back, to stay with us. My mind was full of tangles like cobwebs the devil spun. You have to be silent for an angel to come."

Ma got up to stir the fire and wrap blankets tighter around me.

"All I know is that the devil's gone. He didn't grab my soul, either, although I thought he was going to. I'm back here with you three kids. Where I belong."

Chapter 11
Flood
Spring 1925

Come the next spring, there was a terrible flood. In April it broke suddenly, and without warning. And it came down hard. One moment the skies were spring blue like a robin's egg, and the next moment they were black as night, as if the sky were covered with a blanket. Thunder shook the ground and spun our pots clear off the table. It bounced off one mountaintop and hit another. Devil's breath, they called such thunder up there. Rain fell in gray sheets that hurt as it pelted down. Our road was buried overnight beneath a river of water. The mines were shut down.

It seemed like the end of the world.

We were locked in our cabin for two days. The rain broke through the roof on the first night. Ma set pots everywhere, in the middle of the floor and on top of the stove. She had to drag the beds around so we'd be dry, but a new hole would open up as soon as she did that. Rain pinged into those pots drop after drop, singing us lightly to sleep on the first night; but by the second day, the drops fell so hard it sounded like a shooting gallery.

On the third morning, the sky shone bright blue as if the

whole world were washed clean, Phillip said. Full of diamonds, that air was. Ma dug a trench along the road to channel the water away. She wore Pa's rubber boots that reached up to her hips. She wanted to walk to town, that's why.

"You been cooped up by the weather for two days," she told Phillip, "and all you want is to talk to other folks to see how they made out."

Folks met in town like it was a holiday. The main road into town was washed out. Animals were lost. Roofs had caved in on some of the tenement houses. Leaks sprouted everywhere. The mines were flooded and the men made no wages that week. But nobody seemed to care. Folks just wanted to be with one another.

Phillip said folks blew off steam by trading tales. Soon enough, everyone was laughing about Durka's pig still hiding under his bed. Not even a carrot could coax it out. One woman told how milk straight from her cow turned sour during the storm. Thunder can curdle milk, a man said. He told her to put a rusty nail in the pail to change it back into milk.

Phillip remembered standing with Uncle Matt by the town's loading dock, listening to the roar of that mud brown river as it swirled past, full of belongings it had gobbled up in its path. A white door. Rain barrels. A dead cow. Ma held my hand tightly, for I was known to suddenly bolt off and run away. I had just discovered my running legs at one and a half years old. With Raggedy Ann in my arms, I wanted to explore everything there was to see in Cobalt. I dragged her everywhere.

Everyone stopped talking when the logs rolled by.

They were oak from the largest trees, eight feet thick, hundreds of years old, cracked off at the bottom.

"Mud slide must've knocked those trees down—" a miner started to say.

Folks gasped. The logs had turned over in the current, revealing the men lashed to them with rope. Lumberjacks. Pale swollen bodies rolling over and over in the water.

Nobody moved.

Phillip heard our uncle's voice behind him. "They're long dead. Probably died before they fell into the river."

But someone else cursed.

"Strippin' down all those trees on the mountaintops! Left a trail for the rain to pour in and wash the soil away. That's what yanked those trees out."

"What happened to them, Uncle Matt?" William tugged his sleeve.

"Must have strapped themselves to those big trees when the storm broke loose. Thought they'd be safe. Poor men. Just doing their job."

A shiver must have run through everyone that day. Ma crossed herself and made us do the same. We picked up our supplies at the mining depot and walked back home.

That night we ate our smoked trout and baked potatoes in silence. After dinner, Ma left the stove door wide open. She sat back in her chair, still wearing her apron. She stared into the red glow of that fire for hours, her pile of mending untouched. The fire swirled, running around the wood like it was dancing. Just to watch it made you dream.

She had rocked me to sleep against her chest, the rhythm of her heartbeat like soothing medicine. I drifted in and out. When I took a breath, I felt the two of us were the same person. Afterward, I lay on her lap, asleep, and she left me there, stroking my wavy black hair. I was tiny for my age, so I still fit right in her lap.

There was a stillness around Ma that night that Phillip remembered from the time Pa died. He tiptoed over to her and put his hand upon her shoulder. They were the only ones awake. She looked up, startled at his touch.

"Why, that's just what your pa would have done! Tried to yank me out of my dreaming."

"I wish Pa were here," Phillip said.

"Me too, son."

"Pa would have known what to do. He'd yell to those lumberjacks to warn them and climb up to help just . . . like . . . I keep wondering if someone had come to help him, maybe Pa would have been saved."

Ma reached out her hand and pulled my brother against her.

"Someday, when I'm able to, I'll tell you the story. For now, there's one thing I decided. You and William won't mine and you won't be lumberjacks, either."

"But Ma, that's what men do around here."

"We'll figure something out," she promised. "I've got to have that settlement in my hands before I can do anything. But wherever we go, we will live safe. Even if I have to work my fingers to the bone."

Chapter 12
The Cousins Come
Summer 1925

By June, the ground had finally dried out and a lime green blush spread everywhere. The garlic stalks were high and lettuce was inching up. That's when the cousins came from Croatia. Ma was their sponsor, allowing them to emigrate to Canada. One was Ma's first cousin, Joseph Severenski, from her family's hometown. He left behind a wife and daughter in the old country. He planned to make enough money to bring them over. The other two were brothers, bachelors, Mike and Peter Slivac, second cousins of Ma's. They were all young and ready to work in the mines. They moved into a mining tenement in town.

From the very first moment Joseph stepped into our cabin, something changed. I had never seen such a tall man. He wore farm boots that clunked around and loose overalls like he'd just come in from the barn. His hands were huge. When he petted our heads, his one hand seemed to swallow us. Even his voice was loud in Croatian. It set everyone talking.

But mostly, I felt it in his footsteps, shaking our cabin like the underground drills rattling the tenements. Before he arrived, our home was filled with whispers. We had tiptoed in the dark, clutching tight to one another. We lived in the shadows until he came.

The night before the cousins started work, they ate dinner with us. Coffee was boiling up a storm with more chicory than usual to cut down the caffeine, for the men had to get up early. Croatian miners dropped by to meet them. Some had emigrated from villages and farms surrounding Severin. They all knew people back in the old country. It was as if they were welcoming long lost friends.

But the talk soon turned to mining.

"You go down those tunnels, and soon enough, you'll shed that jacket you got on," one miner said. "Deeper you go, the hotter it gets."

"You'll be sweating bullets in no time. Go slow the first few days, boys, until you get used to it. Pack three big jars of water to drink."

It was then they shushed my brothers and put us all to bed in the back room. But Uncle Matt's voice drifted into Phillip's ears.

"Don't stray away from your partner. Never go down a tunnel alone, even if the boss says it's all right. Let everyone know where you are."

"So they can get to you, son. So they can dig you out in time."

Phillip shivered in the back room. Pa had died down there. My brother never knew how, never dared ask. So he crept out of bed and flattened his ear to the door as they continued.

"We've been working the mines for years, son. Certain things have kept us alive. We look and listen for signs."

"If any of you passes a rabbit before sunup on your way to the mines, it means one thing. Bad luck."

"Never turn around once you go out the door to work, even if you leave your lunch pail behind. You break your luck that way. Better to starve all day than to die."

"I didn't know about all these superstitions," Joe said. "But I heard miners back home don't wash their backs. It could cause a cave-in."

"The birds, boy. We forgot to tell you about the birds! If a bird circles above the mining pit when it's your turn to go down, don't go. None of us would. Birds smell death coming."

"The broken shoes!" Ma said. "The ones Rose dreamed about. But the news came to us too late."

Then their voices no longer spoke in half English and half Croatian, but only in Croatian that my brother didn't totally understand.

"They were speaking about death," my brother guessed. "And whose death could it be but Pa's? They didn't want William or me to hear."

Try as he might, his ear pressed to that door as it was the night they laid Pa out, it was as if the whole world separated him from knowing what had happened to our father.

Phillip would have told me everything, if he knew. He was the pipeline between the world and me. Everything that happened to me flowed through him first. Perhaps that's why I always studied his face. It was bright and full.

I was his shadow. I would have followed him anywhere.

When I was a baby, he was the one who answered my cries and carried me to Ma when she didn't have the strength to pick me up. He always noticed me. After Ma sprang back to life, she seemed too busy with cleaning and baking, gardening, mending and worrying. It was no wonder I trailed after Phillip. He never stopped me either. He just kept going ahead, looking back to coax me on.

I have a memory of the two of us. It's a picture that peeks out at me from the past and it's as clear as daylight. I must have been about two years old then.

I was chasing Phillip, my hands grabbing his coattails, when he began to swing in circles. He pulled me along until we were both spinning. I leaned my head back and looked up. The blue sky was a twirling bowl far above my head like a potter's wheel. Around it, the evergreens reached up so tall, they seemed to touch the sky. I kept holding on to my brother's coat, afraid to let go. My body twisted in every direction. My feet didn't touch the ground. The whole world towered above me.

I was a sapling bending in the wind, clinging to the tree that was my brother.

Chapter 13
Bringing Blessings to a House

Late Summer 1925

From the beginning, her voice led me. I could hardly wait for my feet to hold me up, so that I could follow her. Everywhere. Ma lived in the kitchen, her apron full of flour. I remember pressing my hands against it, big clouds of powdery flour puffing out, whitening my face, making my brothers laugh.

She was always busy with dough, working it until it was warm and soft, like a baby. Her hands sank into it. My fingers, beside hers, poked tiny fingerprints in the dough. Then she covered it up and hid it in a warm spot. Like magic, the dough came to life. It grew and grew. Bubbles popped out all over it like little mouths singing, "Bread! Bread!"

Before she began her day's work, she packed Phillip off to school with lunch in hand, just when the birds stirred. He walked the mile-long road to the one-room schoolhouse in Cobalt. Here and there, other children joined him, spilling out of log cabins in the bush and walking through fall fog or winter snow.

Ma baked on Mondays and Fridays. When I awoke those days, it was to sweet smells in the air. For a year after Pa died, there had been no bread in the cabin. But now Ma rose early and stirred up the sourdough starter, a dried-up crust of yeast she kept in a wooden bowl in a cool corner of the cabin. By late afternoon, loaves of bread and yeast cakes were baked, warm and brown. We smothered slices with jam. William grabbed bites by the handful until Ma slapped his hands away. She always sliced bread with a knife. She never pulled it apart with her hands.

"If you cut it with your fingers, you'll cut your crops in half," she said.

I don't think my brother believed Ma, for behind her back, he yanked off pieces of bread with his bare fingers. We only got a few bites each time, for Ma packed the bread into baskets and loaded them in our wagon. She'd set off for Cobalt, with William and me beside her. She dropped off the baskets at each of the bachelors' tenements, walking in stiffly, picking up the money left on the table, and leaving quickly. No one locked their doors in town. Croatian women stood at the windows like watchdogs, noticing every movement in town, Ma said. After a visit to our aunt, Ma rode by the schoolhouse to bring Phillip home.

Ma and I sat at the table in the late afternoon, chewing slices of warm bread. A tin cup of milk was set for

Raggedy Ann and me, while Ma sipped black tea. She poured it straight out of a teapot. She never stirred the leaves up. As she poured, she explained to me:

"Never stir up tea leaves, Baby. You might stir up changes that you do not want. Only God can change a life, not us. We think we can interfere, but we just make a mess. Once we are born, all that happens to us is as fixed as the stars."

After she drank, she turned her teacup upside down, and then she righted it again. She leaned over it, studying the way the tea leaves lined up. Forming branches like trees. Or a face. Sometimes all bunched up tight like a fist. The shapes told the future, she believed. She liked to wonder about the future.

But I always turned my thoughts around the other way, trying to see the past. To piece our story together. The past stretched out behind me like a mystery road.

I don't think Ma wanted to remember much. Instead, she looked at tea leaves and checked how high the dough rose and stirred the soup. She lived in the little things. For months in my early life, she had sat still, but at her tasks she now moved so fast, my little feet could hardly keep up with her. I saw it in the day-to-day things. She walked steadily toward each new day.

In the afternoon, while Ma cooked, my brothers and I went outside to play. They ran out before me, their cries sharp as coyote calls. I twirled around them like a leaf in the breeze, letting it blow me wherever it pleased. The world was alive. I could feel it in the wind. It blew from unseen places to touch me, then swirled back again into the unknown.

Pa was not the only one who loved the bush. We kids did too. There was a kind of music there, in the bush, that I never heard anywhere else. As if all those evergreen trees and the blue sky sang messages. I remember the sky most. Me, flat on my back, looking up at it. Sometimes, I noticed black clouds bunched up in the north, like Ma's tears trapped inside, pinching her face. For often she moved slowly, a veil of grief pressing down, smothering her. But then the clouds burst and there was rain or snow like quick tears and the sky would clear again. So crystal blue, I thought I could see all the way to heaven.

I could have stayed outside forever—until the dark dusk evening, when the crickets sang and the birds called, sleepy and faint, the warmth of summer sun evaporating.

But then, Ma would call us in, one by one, for bed.

Every Saturday afternoon, she swept with a straw broom, me following her around with a dustpan. She carefully swept from all the corners into my dustpan. When it was full, I carried it outside and threw it to the wind, as she told me to. Once she caught me sweeping the dust right out the open front door.

"Don't sweep straight out the door!" she warned me. "You'll sweep your friends away."

"You'll sweep your money away, too, just while I'm so busy making it," Phillip added. "That's what Pa used to say."

When Ma cleaned, she picked up the bread crumbs

we dropped and threw them out to the birds. From the corners, she plucked the spiders right out of their webs and flung them outside too, hoping they wouldn't inch their way back in. Very carefully she lifted them up, but always left their webs hanging. My brothers laughed when she did that.

"Killing spiders brings rain," she fussed at them. "Breaking their webs breaks your luck."

If Ma accidentally swept a spider into her dustpan, crushing it, I always watched for the rain afterward. Ma's hands moved by themselves as if pulled by strings. Strong, wide hands she had, with a thin gold wedding band. As she kneaded dough with one hand and stirred soup with another, she reminded my brother to collect eggs. All the while, she told me stories about Calumet, in one long breath.

She had to be everyone all at once. And she was.

Chapter 14
The Settlement
April 1926

We had enough to eat and clothes on our back, but nothing more. We lived on the monthly widow's allowance. Ma sewed our clothes from bolts of fabric or gave us hand-me-downs from Aunt Tracey. Ma never threw anything away. From old shirts, torn and too thin for wear, she snipped off buttons and cut out the firm fabric for quilts and patches. Only when the light shone through it as she held it up to the sun would she give in and use it for a dust rag.

All I ever got to wear was my brothers' old jeans and jackets. They never fit me right. Too big and boxy for my skinny arms and legs. All the color faded out. I must have looked like a boy too. Ma cut my dark hair straight around, making it look like a bowl.

The settlement finally came. It was two years overdue. My mother wouldn't touch one penny of it. It was Pa's money. It had to be saved to start up again, as the manager had intended it to be. That's what Pa would have wanted too. So Ma tucked the settlement money safely away in the company bank.

She paced in front of the cabin in the cool evenings

after the money came in, trying to figure out what to do. She was dressed in her long woolen widow's dress with a black wool coat over it, worn thin at the wrists and elbows and the sleeves riding up her arms. She looked like a dark scarecrow searching for a place to stand but never finding one.

You can't talk to Ma about certain things until she's ready. If you want something, you have to watch her. If she's pacing, don't go near her. Same if she's working, hurrying from one task to another like she's outracing the devil. Come by later, when she's resting with her feet up and someone's letter just read in her lap. She'll be gentle then.

The cousins couldn't wait for that. They were in a big hurry. Rushing to get rich. Planning to send for their relatives to join them from Croatia. Eager to buy their own farms and start families of their own. They were always trying to figure Ma out too. They wouldn't let her be.

Joe and the Slivac cousins dropped by on Sundays, their one day off. They thudded into our cabin with their thick black boots. Ma would boil up coffee and pull a poppy seed cake out of its hiding place. They'd sit hours around the table. Sometimes their voices grew loud. Now and again, Joe pounded on the table with his cup. My brother didn't understand most of it, for they spoke in Croatian. It sounded thick and harsh to him compared to the proper English the headmistress spoke in school. Not like the mysterious Latin of the priest either, falling smooth as oil from his lips. But he listened, watching the cousins' faces as they spoke. He began to figure some words out.

"You must leave this place," Joe kept insisting. "There is nothing for you here anymore."

They were the same words the manager had told my mother two and a half years before. She had no voice to say anything then, but she fought the cousins now like a woodchuck had once fought her when she'd cornered it in its den. She stood up at the table and slammed her fists down.

"This is what my husband wanted!" she yelled. "You never met him, so you don't know."

"That's when he could make money here. You can't. You bring in fifteen dollars a month with all the loaves you bake. You have to move on and start again."

"This place is all I have." She gathered up her skirts and stormed out the door.

Ma wasn't willing to listen to the cousins. She wouldn't let go of Cobalt either. But Joe wasn't willing to give up on Ma.

"Frances, you helped us come here. You signed our papers so we could leave the old country. Now we have to help you."

Joe came up with a plan. He saved every cent he made. He ate one meal a day and lived on coffee. He was always searching for ways to make money so that he could buy a farm and send for his family in the old country. He was wide and strong and just beginning in this country. Beside him, Ma looked shriveled and old, though she was just twenty-seven.

"If we stay at the mines, there's only so much money we can make," said Mike. "Only so many hours in a day."

"We heard about a boom in Schumacher, two hundred miles north of here by train," said his brother. "It's a city, not like this small town. We could get jobs in the mines the day we get off the train. They pay more. Those mines are stuffed with gold."

"If we all moved there, we could rent a big house together," Mike offered. "Take on boarders. All the miners go there straight from the old country, with no place to stay."

But it was Joe who said, "You can run it Frances, while we work at the mines. We can all chip in money for the things we'll need to start."

He had remembered Ma's stories about how she'd helped her sister Elsie run a boardinghouse in Detroit before she was married. She was the cook and housekeeper there. She had saved all her money for a wedding gown and honeymoon.

"At night, when we come home from work, we'll help out," promised Peter. "On our days off, we'll work for you."

"I won't go." Ma sank her head down on her arms.

They thought she was stubborn. She was. So they waited. The cousins were stubborn too.

What they did not know was that Pa was still around. We did not talk about it, even to one another, but sometimes, I'd just stand real still outside by the pines and his name filled my mind. He was still a part of us, a spell unbroken.

Ma searched for him one last time. In the summer of 1926, she watched the sky for the clearest, coldest night. She loaded up the shotgun and wrapped us in blankets, and we all sat down on the tree stumps. She leaned the shotgun against a tree within arm's distance. But she soon forgot it was there. She got too busy studying the sky. It was dotted with stars from its ceiling down to the horizon.

Ma pointed up to the stars and called out their names as if she were greeting long lost friends. Bright ones like the North Star. Tiny points dotting a trail to the Big Dipper. Behind the stars were even more stars, layers of them. The Milky Way. She never laughed up at them as Pa had done. She took the light in quietly, as if she were trying to fill herself up with it. Not like my brothers. They whooped it up and threw rocks at the sky, trying to touch the stars. Their voices echoed in the cold night air.

Perhaps they scared the wolves away. On that summer night, no one heard them howl.

I sat on my mother's lap, wrapped in a blanket, and looked up too. She had said that Pa was somewhere up there, in heaven. He was always watching over us, like one of the angels. She thought he was just beyond the stars. But he wasn't.

He was everywhere.

Chapter 15
Leavetaking
September 1926

By September, it had already snowed. We all knew that once winter set in, we wouldn't be going anywhere. Everyone held their breath, waiting for my mother.

Ma seemed to be standing still. For three years, she had tiptoed around the cabin, mourning Pa. She never gave away his coat or boots. They waited, in plain sight, by the door. On the dresser, my father solemnly stared out at us from the wedding photograph propped up there.

Ma had kept the windows shut those three years, although my grandmother in Michigan had taught her to open all the windows wide when someone dies. That way, their spirit can fly straight to God. But Ma wouldn't do it. Not even in the summer, when it was heat heavy. About the cabin, my brother said, there was a stuffy feeling like old quilts and dust.

I never minded. There was a warmth in that Cobalt cabin. A presence watched over me and Raggedy Ann. Her black-button eyes gleamed in the dark at me like bright mirrors, noticing everything. How the shadows fell down and wrapped us both tight. Even in the silence, we were never alone.

Ma harvested the garden instead of listening to the cousins. It was the only place she could think, she said. After the first hard frost, she knelt in the garden like it was a church, yanking up carrots and beets by their wilted heads. Then she dug deep into the dirt with her pitchfork, sifting the soil, as if she were searching for gold. She dug slowly, careful not to nick a vegetable with the prong of her pitchfork. I remember standing by her side when the potatoes floated up like magic from that dirt. I scooped them up in my hands. They were like babies that had left their mother, cold and smooth, smelling of dampness.

This was the only Ma I knew. Wearing a dark house-dress with bare legs and rubber boots to the knees. Huddled in a woolen plaid jacket of Pa's, five sizes too big for her. Digging with her eyes drilled to the ground, her mouth in a flat line, determined to find whatever was buried there.

When I awoke one September morning, the air inside the cabin was chilled. Phillip could hear Ma flying around the rooms like a whirlwind, dragging boxes, yanking clothes out of dressers, pulling suitcases out from under the bed, shaking us in the covers above. For the first time in three years, all the windows were flung wide open, letting in the cold, dry air.

Ma paced restlessly. Her face was flushed as if new blood had started to pump back into her veins.

"We're going to Schumacher with the cousins." She looked over at my brothers stirring. "They're ready to go and so am I."

Phillip's voice stopped Ma. Her busy hands froze in midair.

"Why did you open the windows now?"

"It was time, son. Your pa has to move on. So do we."

"You mean we're going to leave Cobalt and him behind?"

"We're leaving this place, that's all. There is nothing for us here anymore. Joseph is right. But we'll always remember your pa."

My brother kept on. "What if we leave Pa behind and he's forever looking for us? You said yourself that he comes by to visit us here."

"I've had a message. Pa's gone to heaven. He couldn't stay on earth anymore. His time was up."

I sat straight up when I heard those words. Something like lightning crackled up and down my spine. I looked out the window, stunned. Then I noticed the ceiling and the hidden shadows that had always spoken to me. There was nothing up there anymore. Just wooden beams and peeling paint. The cabin seemed deserted.

I remember bolting out the door in my bare feet and pajamas, following Pa's trail, screaming, my arms outstretched to draw him back. Looking up, up to the top of the pines that swayed in the wind. The trees bent over, waving their arms furiously as if something had just passed through them. I raced ahead with open arms. All I wanted was to grab hold of those trees. I felt myself lift up as if I were flying over the treetops, a second behind Pa. He was near, so near, I thought I brushed against him.

But then Phillip caught up with me and scooped me

into his arms. The pine trees swirled furiously and I screamed his name aloud.

"*Pa!*"

The word swept as far as those trees, touching them and disappearing into the thin, cold air. My voice beat against the steep mountains and flung itself back at me, repeating Pa's name against its hard stone sides, echoing in my ears. But it was too late. The trees stood straight up again, their trunks stiff and flat, and everything was still, as if nothing had happened.

I clung to my brother's neck and howled. Nothing could console me.

That afternoon, I cried myself to sleep. When I awoke, the cousins and all our relatives were there, filling the empty shadows with their loud voices. The air was charged with excitement. Ma had told them her decision. Joe and the other cousins would leave ahead of us to look for a house. They'd work at the gold mines and wait for us to join them.

I did not join in the children's games that night, but kept apart, hugging Raggedy Ann to my chest. I had whispered my pain in her ear and she smiled back at me like one of the cemetery angels.

On our last night in Cobalt, the cabin was filled with voices speaking Croatian, miners saying good-bye, tears and handshakes. We ate mounds of mashed potatoes, creamy and buttery with dried dill from the garden. I will never forget the taste of potatoes that grow in Cobalt soil. They are so sweet, they taste almost like whipped cream.

The next morning was gray. We rode in our wagon behind Charley for the last time. All our animals were sold. We headed to the railroad station in the town of Cobalt. Beside me, my two cousins, Helen and Paul, didn't say one word. Helen just cried and yanked on my coat. She knew I was going to leave her, and she must've thought it would be forever. I didn't know anything much about time then, but I remember I cried too, watching her. Aunt Tracey kept pulling Ma's suitcase from her hands to help her, but Ma wouldn't let her.

"We'll come visit at Christmas," our aunt promised through her tears. Her voice, usually loud and gruff, was soft. "We'll cook up a storm just like our mother used to."

Uncle Matt blew his nose and wiped his big eyes behind his dark-rimmed glasses. He set our belongings all in a row. Ten bushels of potatoes and five bushels of carrots and beets stood at our feet beside four suitcases. All that was left of our life in Cobalt.

We stood at the station watching the 1:05 Northland train huff and puff to a stop, with steam clouds blasting so hard out of its guts, they knocked my mother's hat off. She held me to her chest. I hugged her neck tight and wrapped my legs around her.

On board, my brothers pressed their noses to the cold glass window and looked back at the town of Cobalt, shining bright in morning light but shrinking as the train pulled away. Our aunt and uncle and cousins waved until they were just dots. Everything was spinning past me so fast, I felt dizzy. I held still, hoping Pa would join us, but he did not. I clutched Raggedy Ann and squeezed into a ball on my mother's lap.

Ma looked straight ahead at the endless tracks toward Schumacher. Her mouth was tight, her eyes dry. She held her body stiff.

Above our heads, crows pounded the air with sharp black wings, cawing in our ears, *You cannot go back! Ever!*

Schumacher, Northern Ontario

I am forgotten like the unremembered dead.

—Psalm 30 (31)

Chapter 16
Far Away
October 1926

Cobalt was behind us now, shining so bright, like it had its own light. If you asked Phillip about Cobalt, he could go on for hours. Cobalt was a burdock root that grew in all of us. Burdock is the toughest weed there is. It has leaves as big as elephant ears and burrs that stick to your clothes and scratch your skin. Most people try to get rid of burdock. But no matter how deep you dig to yank it out, you'll never kill all its root. That root clings to the soil like a tree stump. Leave one sliver of root, and the plant will break ground again next week.

Schumacher was two hundred miles north of Cobalt, near Timmins—a long day's ride by railroad. The farther north we traveled, the deeper the cold, the blacker the skies. I was sound asleep in Ma's arms the night the Northland pulled into Schumacher. The shrieking of brakes startled me awake. When we stepped off the train at midnight, it was snowing hard in the empty streets. Building after building stood stiff and straight, windows gloomily staring out at us.

I remember the chill. The darkness.

We hurried to our new home, marching behind Joseph in a forlorn line like sleepy soldiers. The boardinghouse was gray shingled, built so close beside other houses that if you reached your arm out a window, you could touch your neighbor's house. All the houses were skinny and tall, a long row of boardinghouses that seemed tired and beaten down. Where the gray shingles had loosened, the boards gaped through like mouths with missing teeth. They looked like giant chicken coops, but they housed heaps of boarders instead of chickens.

I remember looking at the house from the street, frozen to my spot like an icicle. Ma had to carry me. Inside, it was even colder. The floors were bare linoleum without rugs, and there were no drapes as there had been in our Cobalt cabin. In the dining room was a long table that could seat thirty people at a time. Steel folding chairs were propped against the walls. The house echoed with our movements. Our footsteps scuffed against the floor. We dared not even whisper.

We walked through the kitchen, past a stairway. Steps climbed steeply up. Upstairs, the boarders were already sleeping. We had to tiptoe through the house. I shivered in Ma's arms and turned my head toward the softness of her wool coat. Joseph led us to our room at the farthest corner of the house on the ground floor. Ma shut the door tightly behind us, set me in a big bed and lay down beside me. My brothers flopped into the bed next to us. We all fell asleep that night before Ma could undress us.

I never had a chance to ask her anything—what we were doing there or who the boarders were. I had to wait to find out, for the very next morning, Ma wrapped an apron around her black mourning dress and never sat down until bedtime. She set to work scrubbing the house right away. It was empty of boarders during the day, and she moved from room to room, flinging the windows open, scrubbing the floors and walls with pine cleaner. My eyes stung from it. When she was done, the house looked the same to me. Only my mother was changed. Her lips were downturned and her shoulders sagged. Her face paled as gray as the shingles on the house.

From the street outside, long past dark, we heard voices calling and hardy laughter. Twelve boarders burst in the front door with the cousins, joking with one another and clanging their lunch pails down on the kitchen table. Miners and lumberjacks filled the house in no time.

My brothers and I watched them, unseen, from behind a doorway.

What I remember most about the boarders is the noise they brought in. They acted like a hundred brothers let loose from their eleven-hour workday. At the table, they slurped their soup loudly. Ma just stood quietly, serving everyone, and never sat down to eat herself. She watched as the men gobbled down her dinner of fried chicken, cornbread, and a ten-gallon pot of chicken soup with dumplings.

"Men from the old country always have to start a meal with soup," she told us. "A meal's not a meal without it."

After dinner, there was a slowness to the boarders. They pushed away from the table, groaning over their stuffed bellies, squeaking their metal chairs against the hard floor, and trudged to the sitting room. They puffed on cigarettes, filling the house with smoky clouds. The talk grew quieter and quieter. Finally, by eight-thirty, they crawled upstairs to their beds like slugs.

"Work. Food. Sleep," Ma said. "That's what boarders crave."

The men stumbled past us. A few patted our heads, mumbling good night to my mother, but most drifted upstairs without a word. The Slivacs disappeared too. They shared a room with Joseph off the dining room. Joseph and Ma sat up for hours that first night, talking in the kitchen. Their voices drifted into my ears, steady, insistent, buzzing louder and louder like angry bees. But it was my mother's voice that surprised me the most. Hers was the loudest.

I lay in bed, alone. Ma seemed miles away, though she was just in the kitchen. Our room, at the back of the house, was the coldest spot. We were away from the center of the house, where the heat radiated from the wood furnace, and far from the kitchen, where the cookstove was always lit. On winter nights in that bedroom, you could see your breath steam up the air.

Finally, in pitch blackness, Ma climbed into bed beside me. She sighed deeply, pulling her knees tightly to her chest as if trying to hold herself together. She stroked my head so softly, it was almost like a tickle. She fell asleep instantly but I did not.

I shivered beneath all the feather comforters piled on

top of me. Whatever blessings I had known in the bush had been torn away. The tall pines. A presence looking over me. The wind. Even the stars. I told myself never to look up to them now. I knew I would not find Pa there anymore.

Cobalt was a long way off.

Chapter 17
Miners and Lumberjacks
Late Fall 1926

The men woke in darkness. Deep dark. Four A.M. When the dreams lay upon me, thick as vapor. I opened my eyes and knew she was gone. The spot beside me, where my mother had lain, was empty and cold, but still imprinted with the shape of her body. She hardly took up any space at all. She knew she couldn't lie there long. The house came alive while I lay hidden in my blankets. My dreams disappeared, and no matter how hard I tried, I couldn't call them back.

The men were already up and moving around. I could hear them in the rooms above me. Early morning sounds. Coughing. Spitting. The teakettle boiling for hot shaves. Water splashing. Ma's footsteps clunking up the staircase as she carried water. Her slow footsteps down the steps as she carried out chamber pots from the night. Doors slamming as chamber pots and shaving pots were flung and emptied into the cold morning air and then clanged down on the back porch. Boots stomping down the stairway. Voices gathering into a brawl by breakfast time. When it was still dark outside, the boarders left for work in a flurry of movement.

My brothers vanished too, every day. They both dressed in Sunday clothes: gray flannel knickers, knee-socks and pressed white shirts. They slicked back their hair, ready for school. They bolted outside, fighting off Ma's attempts to check if their faces were scrubbed red. I wished I could jump inside their book bags, along with their sandwiches, books and rulers, and follow them wherever they went. When they slammed the door, the house suddenly seemed enormous. It became a house of work. I had nothing to do but trail behind Ma, until she shooed me away.

I'd peek out the curtains in the afternoons, watching the hillside. If only I could have gone to the forest then, while everyone was busy. Stand among the trees and pretend I was one of them. Cover myself in a blanket of snow and spend the day breathing in the sharp air. But the woods were far off. They were not just outside the door, as they had been in Cobalt, but distant, unreachable. No one had time to take me there. All I could do was silently wait for my brothers to return.

But as soon as they'd come home, Ma had chores for them to do: sweep the kitchen floor, carry laundry upstairs and cart wood from out back into the cellar. Just before dinner, they both sat down at the kitchen table to do homework. I'd yank Phillip's arm to play but he wouldn't budge. He kept his eyes down on the page and wrote marks in a black composition book. He was serious about homework. Not William. He'd flip through the pages of his book and whistle until Phillip finished.

"You're so smart, Phillip. The top of the class, Miss Mandy said today," he coaxed. "Can you help me look as smart as you?"

"Do your own homework," muttered my big brother.

"You wanna have a dumb brother? C'mon, do these math problems for me."

Phillip looked like he wanted to swat him but William whispered, "If you get up from the table now, Ma will give you another job to do. Keep writing and she'll leave us both alone."

We all sneaked a look at our mother, stirring up beef barley soup in a ten-gallon pot, her hair frizzed up, her face lost in clouds of steam. Phillip frowned but he took the book William shoved at him and figured out all the answers. William sat back, grinning from ear to ear.

I had to wait for Ma too. I'd tug at her apron to make her sit down with me.

"Just let me finish the pie dough, Baby. I have to get it in the oven before six so it'll be piping hot at seven for dessert."

But after the pie dough came last-minute preparations for dinner, and by then the men burst through the door. Ma always smiled and nodded at them, coaxing them with more food. Maybe she felt sorry for them. To me, the men were stray animals that had wandered in from the wild.

Sometimes a boarder or two ate with us. William named one of them Goldilocks. His beard was so red and rusty, it looked like it'd been dipped in gold. It wiggled up and down when he talked. William kicked my foot under the table whenever Goldilocks slurped his soup. I pressed my lips together and tried not to look, but I always peeked. His beard dipped into his bowl, dripping greasy soup all over his shirt. He'd just wipe it with the back of his hands, smack his lips and sigh.

"Best soup I ever tasted, Mrs. Chopp." He'd grin, toothless above his red beard.

To me, miners and lumberjacks were all alike. But my brothers had a way of telling them apart. They were the authorities on boarders.

"They're both filthy," Phillip said. "Black with mud from head to toe. Most of 'em don't even bother to scrub till Saturday night."

"If you put them side by side," William swore, "the lumberjack is taller. Sunburned too. He wears layers of clothes: long underwear poking out of a plaid woolen shirt. Even in winter, climbing hills and axing trees, he's steaming hot and peels off layers of clothes like an onion."

"The miner goes down deep," Phillip explained. "The deeper he goes, the hotter it gets, so he doesn't pile on clothes."

From the sitting room at night came laughter, loud as a lion's roar.

"Lumberjacks are loud," William said, laughing. "They're used to yodeling to their partners off in the hills, where they can't see them."

"When they come into a room, they swing their arms around," Phillip added. "But miners curl up like they're still in some hole in the ground."

I knew one thing they forgot. "All of them sleep like logs."

My brothers roared at that one. At night we could hear them snoring, a full story above us, like they were all cutting logs.

Soon enough, Ma gave me a job. I made the beds in our room, standing on the bed to yank the heavy feather comforters straight. She didn't care if the beds were perfect, as long as they were smoothed down. Afterward, I played with my Raggedy Ann doll, folding pieces of cloth around her soft body to make a pretend dress. She was the one who always stayed by my side, the only piece of Cobalt I could still touch. Like me, she wore hand-me-downs and waited in cold rooms and on steps for the housework to be done. She knew all my secrets. Her black-button eyes probed right through me, knowing everything.

I often sat with her in my favorite spot, on the bottom step of the staircase facing a bright window of stained glass. It was the only pretty thing about that house. In the late afternoon, just before my brothers came home from school, the sun hit that window fully. It cast colored rays of light onto the stairs. Ruby red. Cobalt blue. Golden amber. I'd sit in those rays and bathe myself in their rainbow of colors. The sun warmed me through and through even on bitter cold winter afternoons.

I'd close my eyes and drift. Everyone was far away, busy at school, in the mines or in the kitchen. We only heard from Aunt Tracey by letter, never her voice, never her laughter anymore. I drifted all the way back to Cobalt. In my mind, I'd see our cabin, so real I felt I could reach my hand out the window and touch the evergreens.

I began to daydream all the time.

Chapter 18
Boss of the Boardinghouse
Winter 1927

The days grew shorter and darker. Our relatives in Cobalt did not come to visit us at Christmas, as they had promised. I do not remember that holiday. It came and went like any other day. All I remember that winter is how the boarders dragged themselves home from the gold mines in pitch black.

One winter night, Ma had a ten-gallon pot of beef stew ready with yeast buns, baked potatoes and pumpkin pie with fresh whipped cream. The cousins had to help her serve it, for the men were seated almost as soon as they came in the door. They had smelled it all the way down the street. The boarders ate silently, dipping buns in their bowls. Everyone had seconds and thirds until that big pot was empty. Ma stood by as they talked.

"You didn't say your cousin could cook, Joe." One patted his belly. "I'm so stuffed, I won't need to eat for days."

"Bet you'll be the first one at the table come breakfast," said another, laughing.

Ma watched them, frowning. Not one of the men spoke directly to her. The men sat back in their chairs, smoking and talking, while she washed the dishes and the Slivacs shoveled the walks outside. It was late when Ma called Joe into the kitchen.

"There's more work here than I can do, Joe. You can't help out—"

Joe tried to interrupt her but Ma drilled him silent with her eyes.

"I didn't get the laundry done this week. It's piled up in heaps. The cleaning alone takes all day and the shopping too. I'm going to do what we did in Detroit when I worked with Elsie. Hire some maids. Send the laundry out. Have fresh food delivered. I'll do the cooking."

Joe was up on his feet in no time.

"How can we make money if we hire help?" he shouted at her.

"I am one woman!" Her voice rose up and so did she, a foot and a half shorter than him, yet somehow taller. "Once folks learn how fine I keep this house, more boarders will come. Then we'll make that money you talk about."

The very next day, Ma and I walked to the neighbors up and down the boardinghouse row, looking for hired help. I peeked out at Schumacher from behind the scarf tied tightly around my face. The wind whipped at my face so hard, it sucked my breath away. There was no wild bush there, though I could see it off in the distance. Evergreens stood frozen stiff on the hills. They did not wave to me. All the trees around us had been cut down to make way for the city. On the main street, stone buildings rose up like statues, huge and forbidding, not like the hand-built log cabins in Cobalt. The sidewalks bustled with people walking in every direction, wearing their best clothes in the middle of the week—fancy shawls, hats and coats. Their eyes were set on the buildings up ahead, their minds busily wrapped up in their own thoughts. They walked so fast, I thought they would knock us down.

I remembered how in Cobalt, all the faces were familiar. If my mother didn't know someone's name, it was because they had just arrived. She knew in which cabin folks lived and how many kids were in each family. Here everyone was a stranger. We were nobody. Not the Chopp family. Not Croatians. Everyone passed us by without a nod in this boomtown.

Ma soon asked Mr. Lee to pick up our bags and bags of laundry. She hired two red-faced maids, Erin and Maureen, teenage sisters with Irish accents. Maureen was the older of the two, with thick wavy hair piled on top of her head, curls dangling in her eyes as she worked, wide-hipped and plump.

"You're young," Ma told them. "You can run up and down that staircase all day. I can't."

And so they did. They cleaned the rooms and helped with the cooking. The house soon began to run like a hotel. The cousins helped too, stoking the wood furnace, hammering nails, and patching holes in the ceiling. Within a month, thirty boarders sat around the dining room table. We ate in shifts, the boarders first. Our family, with the cousins and maids, ate afterward. The men were Irish,

German, French, Italian and Croatian. Ma learned to make soda bread, bacon, meatballs and spaghetti with home-made sauce.

Each night as the men ate, they traded stories or recipes.

"You never saw a tree crack down to the ground like that one," boasted Pierre LeFleur.

"Sauce got to be heavy," insisted Tony Adoranti. "You wanna cook lots of chicken fat with a big handful of garlic. Slip in some red vino too, missus."

Ma and the boarders worked together. But to my brothers and me, the boarders lived on one side of a fence and we on the other, although we lived in the same house. The men didn't take much notice of us kids. We lived in their shadow. But we observed them every chance we got.

After dinner, while the men talked in the sitting room, we'd sneak peeks of them from around the corner. Smoke drifted out in clouds from cigars, pipes and cigarettes. The boarders did something disgusting then. They cleared their throats loudly, like they were gargling. Then they'd spit into brass spittoons set at their elbows. It sounded like their insides were going to blast out of them. They'd aim their spit right into those spittoons. Gobs of it. They never missed once.

"Bullseye!" William called out each time we heard a pinging sound.

One evening, Grizzly Bear heard us giggling in the hallway. You would never want to meet that man in the woods. He was a French lumberjack, so tall he stooped to get in the door. He was always opening his shirt and rolling up his sleeves to show off his muscles. His biceps were bigger than a grown man's head.

Grizzly Bear stomped out of the sitting room, towering over us like a tree. William was making the worst noises at the time. Grizzly Bear grabbed my scrawny brother and carried him off under one arm into the sitting room, his legs kicking.

"This kid wants to learn to spit like us," he announced to the other boarders. "Shall we teach him?"

Phillip and I watched with wide-open mouths. We hesitated in the doorway, wanting to run and tell Ma but knowing that if we did, we'd all be in plenty of trouble. Meanwhile, the men gargled and spit into the spittoons. Spit flew through the air and landed with wet plops in the spittoon beside William's head. His eyes bulged out of his face.

"Your turn!" boomed Grizzly Bear.

"I can't," my brother squeaked. "You're choking me!"

The boarder loosened his arm around William's waist so that he could wiggle out a bit but not get free. My brother started to gargle and pump up his chest. We heard a loud puff of air. The biggest gob of spit we ever saw flew out of William's mouth and landed in a gooey mess in the spittoon.

The men clapped and cheered. Grizzly Bear set my brother down.

"Just beginner's luck, kid," he sneered.

William was a pip-squeak beside him, his hair blown back and his thin face white. But he looked the boarder straight in the eye, dropped another gob in the spittoon and walked out of the room without a word.

"He's gonna pay for that," William swore to us afterward.

"You were just lucky you knew how to spit," Phillip told him.

"Yeah!" I added. "And that Ma didn't find out."

If the men wanted something special, like a shirt pressed for Sunday mass or their shoes shined, they never asked Joseph. They went to Ma. She'd get it done. But my mother had rules for the boarders to follow too. They weren't allowed to smoke in their rooms. Only in the sitting room were there ashtrays. Before we arrived, one of the boardinghouses had burned to the ground because a boarder had been smoking in bed. Ma was scared to death of fire. She said those boardinghouses leaned together like pages in a book and would go up in flame just as easily. No drinking, either, in any room, was her order too. Ma was the boss of that house.

Ma was rooted to the ground like a stubborn chicory root, thick and wiry, that no one could yank out. No matter that she was whittled to a thin stalk and nothing bloomed on her anymore—no flower, no green leaf—she stood up stiff and straight, pitting herself against dry ground.

After the boarders went upstairs at night, silence fell over the house. Ma worked in the kitchen with my brothers.

They tiptoed about their work, emptying buckets and gathering garbage. I'd sit in my spot on the bottom step of the oak stairway. The staircase led up so steeply that it might as well have been a mountain. Only if you had long legs like a lumberjack, I thought, could you climb them. I'd look up that stairway and think I could never go up. Ever. So I'd sit alone in the quiet the boarders had left in a trail behind them.

The house felt strangely empty, like it didn't belong to anyone. We had to make our life around the boarders. Even when they noisily filled the dining room, you knew it wasn't home, but more like a hallway folks passed through on their way somewhere important, leaving us behind.

Outside, it was deep dark and wind howled down the chimney. Snow fell down endlessly. I huddled with a draft at my back, hugging Raggedy Ann. We were the only girls in a house of men, so thin and dark, we could have been mistaken for shadows on the stairway.

I remembered a girl in a fairy tale that Phillip once read to me. She was spirited into the woods by evil men. Behind her, she secretly dropped a trail of breadcrumbs so that her family could follow. She was found in the end.

But I had nothing to leave in my trail. I had left everything behind.

I once lived in a place where the spirits swirled. But it was empty now. Full of echoes.

Chapter 19
Waiting
Winter 1927

The days ticked by. There was never a pause, never a moment for Ma and me together. On Sundays, after a big lunch for the boarders and while they talked and the maids cleaned up, Ma took a few hours off. She wrote letters and paid bills. She'd sew up Raggedy Ann, for her insides were always falling out, and mend my brothers' pants. Afterward, she'd stretch out on the bed, and in the middle of a sentence she'd fall asleep.

There was only one place I dreamed of going then: up to the forest that grew all around Schumacher, tiptoeing out without being seen. Perhaps I'd find something there, the magic I'd lost in Cobalt. But I could not go anywhere alone. Everyone was too busy to take me. I didn't even bother to ask. The muffled voices of the boarders traveled from the dining room. My brothers' laughter trailed from the yard where they helped the cousins. And I held still and quiet in the darkened bedroom.

No one talked about Pa anymore. It was as if we'd left him in his grave in Cobalt and moved on without him. His photograph sat on Ma's dressing table, his brown eyes watching us, but no one looked back except me.

Both my brothers remembered Pa. His presence had filled the cabin, making the wild bush smaller. To William, Pa was a dim figure, trudging home after dark with his steel lunch pail clinking like a cow bell just before he came in the door. Pa was a toss in the air on a bright summer afternoon in 1923. William had that to hold on to.

Phillip had more than memory. He had my father's name and looks: his thick hair and wide chest. A quietness. In his mind, he had a clear picture of our father, for he had looked upon him every day for six years. Pa looked back at him too, the firstborn son, and I am sure he smiled. My big brother always waited up until Pa came home from his fourteen-hour workdays. If he drifted off, he'd awaken when he heard the door creak open. Even on that night when the miners carried him home, Phillip waited up to see Pa one last time. He alone remembered the candlelight shining on his still, pale face.

Phillip said our pa was black soot from head to toe when he came home from the mines. Just his eyes shone through like stars.

All I have is stories, bits and pieces of him.

I hounded Phillip with my questions. I asked him why Ma never spoke about Pa anymore. My brother was nine then, the oldest kid I knew.

"She can't," he said. "She misses him too much."

"But I miss him too and all I wanna do is talk about him."

"You miss him 'cause you never knew him. But Ma misses him in a different way."

"How?"

"She misses waiting for him to come home at night and how he took care of everything. Now she's alone."

"But we help her."

"Not like Pa. He was the boss. That's the way it was when they were together."

Together. I'd never thought of Ma and Pa together, only about Pa as my father. My brother said they'd loved each other right from the start and that's how it was supposed to be. I could never imagine anyone being the boss of Ma, either, not even a man. Joe had tried and it didn't work.

"There's a pit inside her like in the mines," my brother said, looking away. "Where Pa used to be."

I had never heard my mother laugh. Only a few times did I remember her smiling. I had the same feeling inside me. It never went away.

I couldn't tell anyone about it, not even my mother.

She had become a sphinx. I'd seen a picture of one in my brother's history book, the kind there are in Egypt. It rose straight-backed and stiff, its eyes unblinking, its features flat. All its feelings and all its treasures were shoved down into secret tunnels inside. No one could enter it. In the absence of tears, it had turned to stone.

If we had said Pa's name, she would have come undone.

I was always the first one to bed, sitting so long on the bottom step that I was almost sound asleep, dreaming, my head fallen against the wall. But as soon as my mother dragged me to bed, I'd sit up and wait for my brothers. They raced each other into the bedroom, whacking pillows at each other's heads. They'd explode with gasps at what the other guy had done and chase each other around the room, leaping from bed to bed. Until Ma came in to check on them. Then they lay down and pulled their covers up, but I could tell they were still kicking each other beneath them.

Soon as I saw Ma, something leaped inside me.

Tell me. Tell me . . . about . . . Pa.

The words sat right there on the tip of my lips, trembling, but I never said them aloud. Instead, I'd close my eyes and let Ma kiss us all good night, shut off the lights and tiptoe back to her work.

Her footsteps echoed down the hallway. From the kitchen, I'd hear the clinking of glasses and the metal ringing of pots as she put the dishes away. The bedroom filled with the sound of my brothers' deep long breaths. They had fallen asleep in mid-fight, their arms dangling off the side of the bed, mouths wide open.

But I'd try anyway.

"Phillip?" I called across the room.

Sometimes he'd awaken and tell me one more story about school, or Cobalt, if I begged him.

No answer.

"William?" I called louder.

They were both sound asleep. I'd lie awake, my feet frozen, wanting just one thing: for my mother to come back.

She was a long time coming.

I always fell asleep waiting for her. I'd awaken when she crawled into bed, no matter how quietly she tried to move. I'd wiggle close to her, feeling her warmth against me on those nights that were forever cold in Schumacher. She'd stroke my hair, softly stretching each strand, putting me to sleep. Her touch reached inside me, to a place no word could name. Sometimes, I pressed my head against her chest and listened to her beating heart. I loved the rhythm of it. It ticked away slow and steady, loud in my ear.

Her sorrow enveloped me like a cloud, yet it took me in and soothed me too, for then I did not feel so alone. Even if she wouldn't talk about Pa or Cobalt, I knew they were there.

My mother was soon asleep, her arms flung out of the covers. Her breathing joined my brothers', filling the room with clouds of sleep. To Ma, the boardinghouse was like a train. Once she got on board and it started down the tracks well before dawn, she wouldn't get off until bedtime.

I never got the chance to ask her anything. I had to make Pa up myself.

Chapter 20
Awakening
Late Winter 1927

Angel of God, my guardian dear
To whom God's love commits thee here
Ever this day, be at my side
To love and guard, to rule and guide.
Amen.

A single moment turned our lives around.

One night while I slept, I was awakened by great heat as if the summer sun rose in the middle of the night. I stared all around. Light fell over my covers. Not like sunlight, which is bright, or lamplight, which is soft. Not like any light I had seen before. Blinding. Of a whiteness as see-through as gauze. I looked above me. Something was forming, twirling from spun gold and sky blue threads, until it formed an image, covering the wall from the ceiling down to the bedpost. It was so startling that at first I felt pinned to the mattress.

It was neither man nor woman, yet seemed to be both. Its hair was flowing and golden, reaching its shoulders. It wore a long garment like a dress that swirled as if there were a night wind. About its waist was a wide gold band. In its hands, it held long-stemmed flowers. Its eyes were windows of light. At its back rose two great wings with snowy feathers. Though it towered above me, and no one was awake but me, I crept toward it until I sat at its feet looking up. It turned to me then and with its outstretched hands, blessed me. All its light poured into me. I was warm and yellow-bright with light in that cold winter room.

I remember standing up, talking and even laughing aloud. From all sides, I began to hear the questioning voices. Doors opening. Footsteps pounding on the floor. Someone lit the bedside candle.

"What is it, Baby?" called my mother's worried voice.

Then a man's voice, maybe Joseph's. "What is the child doing?"

But their voices seemed far away. I stood in a halo of pure light. It held me to the figure as if we were in another world. I stared as long as I could, until the figure grew hazy. I called out to it. But the gold faded, and as it did, I reached my hands up.

Ma's hands circled my outstretched arms.

"What do you see there on the wall?"

I found my voice then. "It's leaving!"

Even as I spoke, the darkness closed in around me. In the last light, I described the figure on the wall. I sat beside my mother, surrounded by my dumbstruck brothers and all the cousins standing in their striped pajamas and nightcaps, scratching their heads. By the time I was done, the light was gone, the wall blank and the plaster as uneven as it was before. The cold night air penetrated my skin.

"What was it, Ma?" I begged her. "It wore a dress and its hair was spun of gold."

She was rocking me back and forth, folding me into her. Her eyes were huge bowls of blue in her face.

"Don't you know, Baby?" she whispered. "An angel has come to you!"

Everyone stared at her.

She told the cousins to go back to bed then, that I would be all right. They padded softly down the hallway in their slippers. My brothers were ordered under the covers, but they both peeked out at Ma and me. She stroked my hair, strand by strand, stretching it out long and free, so that it felt beautiful, like the angel's.

"You have been so unhappy since we left Cobalt. Don't think I haven't seen it. The angel has come to remind me."

"She always begs us to tell her stories about Pa," Phillip piped up. "But I don't know all of 'em."

My mother studied me. "Is that true?"

I nodded.

"Why didn't you just come and ask me—" She paused. "Never mind. I haven't stopped a minute. What do you want to know about your pa?"

The question hung there, shining in midair. I had a most delicious feeling, like summer sun swirling in the pit of my stomach.

"Tell me . . . Tell me what you remember most."

Her eyes looked around the room. All our dark eyes were set upon her, eating her up. She swallowed.

"The best part was when your pa was in the cabin with us. He filled the bush up. But what I remember most is how I waited for him to come home. When I heard his boots on the porch, I felt safe. I had everything I wanted with your pa."

Her long copper hair was loose. Gray strands shone in it like the silver in the mining tunnels. Worry streaks, she called them. I reached up to touch them, wishing I could change them back into copper. We saw her tears then, falling without end, sprinkling over my face until they mixed with my own and my brothers' too, for they had tiptoed out of bed to join us. We could not tell which tears were our mother's and which were ours. They were all mingled.

Chapter 21
Down in the Mines
June 1927

When the warning whistle blew that afternoon, Ma was standing at the sink, scrubbing potatoes. Her hands were suspended as she listened. I watched how the whistles shivered through her, making her remember.

Maureen wiped her hands on her apron and looked out the window. "Five whistles!" she screamed. "Something's happened in the mines! They're warning all the men to get out."

She burst out the door in her apron, her bright face suddenly ashen.

"She's got a sweetheart working those mines," Erin told us.

But Ma hadn't heard the girls. She spoke in a flat voice to no one.

"There must have been a whistle that day. But I never heard it, a mile away in the bush. Though I felt it, all through me, when the crows flew by."

She did not budge from the sink. I went over to her and slipped my fingers into her cold, wet hands.

There was a rumble from the city that rattled the dishes in the sink. Then a stillness came that settled over us like a cloud. I could almost see the miners we knew, all the cousins and the boarders, trapped underground, each one looking up through the darkness, wishing for sky. I thought I heard the air whisper Pa's name.

Ma turned back to the half-washed potatoes.

"The miners may come back at any time," she said, sighing. "They'll be cold and hungry. I have to get this meal cooked."

It was an emergency in Schumacher. My brothers came home early from school. They both watched and waited for any sign of a miner on his way home, but the streets were empty. They begged Ma to let them go to the mining pits, but she shuddered.

"Don't ask me again or I'll send you both to your room."

Dinner was ready long before the boarders trudged home. Late that evening, we heard their slow, heavy footsteps. They walked in so black with soot, we did not recognize them. Their mouths hung flat and sour, their faces unshaven. About their clothes clung the smell of smoke.

They did not sit down.

Ma scanned them nervously. Only half the boarders came home. Familiar faces were missing. It wasn't until an hour later when Joseph walked in with the Slivacs that Ma breathed out a deep sigh.

Mike patted Joseph's shoulder. "Joseph got out just in time, Frances. After the whistle blew, there was time for five elevators to bring the men up. He was on the last one."

"A fire broke out in one of the tunnels," Joseph explained. "Then it lit up the kerosene tanks and exploded.

The whole town shook. The mines caved in right beneath the street."

Peter looked around. "Some of your boarders are still helping dig men out. But it's dangerous. Another cave-in can happen any moment."

"Who is missing?" Ma wrung her hands.

"At roll call, many men did not answer. We worked all evening, digging men out. Found thirteen. But more are still missing."

"The ones you found?" Erin begged them.

"All dead but three, miss. Suffocated in those blasted tunnels."

"And Billy, Maureen's sweetheart?" she asked. "Is he out?"

"He's one of the lucky ones. But Kolich was not found, or Legedza."

We all looked at one another. They were our boarders.

"Will you wake us at three A.M. and make breakfast?" Joseph asked Ma. "Ten of us have volunteered to return to the mines to dig."

Ma nodded.

Dinner was silent that night. We all ate together. Around us, emptiness sat in the chairs like ghosts. Reminders. Somewhere, the missing men were trapped in darkness. The cousins left in the middle of the night to help. By morning, five more bodies had been discovered. Each time they found a miner, the church rang its bells, tolling to the families to come and claim their loved one. It tolled all that day.

That night, it seemed the whole city showed up at the Catholic church, a few streets away. The small church was packed. Families squeezed side by side into the pews and in the aisles and stood at the back. Worried mothers with babies clinging to them. Here and there, rescued miners, coming to give thanks. Everything was in shadow. From the darkened corners, the statues of the saints stood frozen, their hands lifted in blessing, their faces illuminated by candlelight. The words of the mass in that cold, dark church beat inside me. We began to sing. Whatever we had squeezed in our hearts, the grief, the memories, fell out our open mouths. Answering the priest's prayers. *Amen.* Repeating the chants. *Gloria Patri et Filio et Spiritui Sancto.* Up into the air above us, swirling in the clouds of thick incense. Rising higher and higher on their journey to heaven. *Alleluia.*

The mines were closed for a week. Each day, the miners dug up more men. Some had survived, the ones they dug out on the second and third days, though their limbs were crushed and their lungs damaged. But there was no sign of our two boarders. They had worked side by side on the day of the fire.

"Is there any chance for them?" Ma asked as the days went by.

Joseph shook his head. "There's no air down there. No food. Not a drop of water. It'd be hard for anyone to make it. Most we've pulled out did not survive the fire."

Each day, the numbers increased. The church bells

tolled again and again. On the seventh day, the count had reached thirty-nine men. Legedza had been dragged out dead. Just as the officials were standing around, discussing how long to continue digging, shouts rang out. A miner's leg had been uncovered and it had moved. Everyone descended into the pits in spite of fear of more cave-ins. That day, they pulled out Kolich. His arms and ribs were broken but he was alive. He had sucked on shoe leather and drunk his own urine to survive.

That night, all the miners sat up late in the dining room. Some argued that there must have been a warning on the day of the fire, an omen. Perhaps a bird flew above the pits and no one saw, one said. There is always a sign, said another. Why did we not see anything, then? someone yelled.

In the midst of the men's argument came our mother's thin voice. It silenced them all.

"I wonder if he heard them. There's not a day that goes by but I don't wonder."

One of the Slivac brothers broke the silence.

"There was no time, Frances. I pray your husband didn't hear it. He was too far out in that tunnel to make it back to the shafts anyway. They say it stretched a mile out. Maybe God let him die in peace, not knowing what hit him."

None of the boarders had heard the story of the Cobalt cave-in.

Neither had we kids. Everyone stared at Ma.

She turned to us and sighed. "It's time you knew."

She nodded at Joseph to continue.

"Your pa was working the one-man drill," Joseph said in a flat voice.

All the miners nodded and murmured.

"That's what did it," he continued. "He drilled by himself with no partner to watch out for him. Miners should never let that happen. If he'd have been closer to the shaft too, he would have been saved."

"We wouldn't allow that now. But miners had no rights back then," a boarder said.

"The company made a profit that way," explained Joe. "They paid one man instead of two to drill. There's a law against it since we started a union."

In the silence that followed, my older brother asked our cousin, "But what was the sound Pa was supposed to hear?"

"The miners swore that just before the cave-in that day came knocking. Hammers pounding deep underground, hard and steady. The men on top ran out just in time. The walls caved in behind them."

"What was knocking?" one of the lumberjacks asked.

"The Knockers. They've helped miners for centuries. Like angels, they are. Some give warning by hitting hammers. Others give clues about where to find the silver or gold."

"I heard 'em once," one miner said, nodding. "Tapping in a wall in front of me. When I set my pickax to it, I dug into a vein of silver so deep and wide, I was at it for months."

Joseph looked at Ma. "Matt says Phillip was found in the same spot as his drill and bucket. He had not moved. He did not hear the warning, then. Otherwise, he would have run. God let him die in peace. They say his face looked gentle when they brought him up."

My mother dabbed her eyes with a handkerchief. "It's what I'd like to believe, but it's always been a mystery to me. I couldn't even tell my children what happened. The shame of it. That he should have been so deep in that tunnel all alone."

It was then a memory sprang up in Phillip. He told everyone how he remembered Pa sitting him on his lap one night, his serious brown eyes upon him. He thought he was telling him a bedtime story.

"Snow White had these friends—the seven dwarfs," Pa had told him. "I hear them sometimes in the mine, son."

"What do they do in the mines?" Phillip had asked.

"Ever see what those dwarfs carry? Pickaxes. Crowbars. Lunch pails. Hammers. They're miners. They live underground. Tap where there's a wide vein of silver. Once they left me a gift."

Pa pulled a shiny rock out of his pocket.

"On my way home yesterday, I felt something heavy in my pocket. Found this. It's pure silver, son. Those dwarfs must have slipped it into my pocket while I was busy hammering away."

After Pa was buried, Phillip searched through all of Pa's pockets for that chunk of silver, but he never found it.

Our mother smiled at his story, but her eyes were brimming with tears. She hugged us all good night, telling us that our pa did not suffer. I kissed the tears on her thin face and then tiptoed into bed, my mind lit up with my brother's words. I lay awake a long while, whispering to Raggedy Ann, the two of us trying to arrange the pieces of the puzzle of that day, but nothing seemed to fit.

That night, I dreamed of Pa in a tunnel in the deep dark belly of the earth, a long mile out. He was hammering at a wall, bits of metal quicksilvering in his lantern's glow. Then the knocking began. Faint at first. Far away. Pa slammed his drill down so hard into the rock, he did not hear it. But then he looked up, his drill silent, listening.

This time he heard.

He took his hat off and pushed back his hair with sooty hands. His dark head gleamed with silver flakes. Down they fell to the ground, sparkling and dancing everywhere. He was not alone as they all say he was. Seven others swung their axes at the wall beside him, blinding him with their light. Messengers.

Pa set his drill to the wall again. He had hit a fat vein of silver that gleamed two feet wide in the dirt.

You should have seen his face. It was the first time I ever saw it.

It was gentle, like Joseph said, and handsome. He was smiling. He did not know that the walls had caved in around him.

Chapter 22
Full House
Fall 1927

We had lived in the boardinghouse for a year when the cousins hammered a sign on the front shingles: Full. Fifty-two boarders lived with us. The bedrooms were jammed. Men even slept in the hallways upstairs. New-comers were always knocking on our front door, looking for a room.

"It's your cooking, Frances," the cousins teased my mother. "Goulash. Chicken paprikash. Pierogies. Wild blueberry pie. Miners sniff it cooking all the way from the pit and come running."

We now ate in three shifts around the dining room table. The longest-staying boarders ate first, then the newer boarders, and finally, us. By that time, it would be eight o'clock. Our stomachs were growling. Sometimes, the cousins fell asleep at the table, heads falling onto their plates. After a long day at the mines, they had to stoke the wood furnace and shovel snow too. They never sat down until dinnertime. Ma woke them up to go to bed.

On Sundays, the cousins worked in a smokehouse they'd built in the backyard. They smoked homemade kielbasa and blood sausage hung on strings above a choking fire. Blood sausage was so greasy, it left a ring around your mouth. William swore it was made from pig's blood and rice, but I ate it anyway. My brothers had to pile up wood before and after school to keep that fire burning. If you stepped into the smokehouse, the smoke clung to your clothes and hair like skunk spray.

Ma was in charge of the sauerkraut and pickle barrels on the back porch. They filled the house with garlic and dill odors. Each morning, she poked a wooden spoon into the barrels, stirring things up, until the pickles and sauerkraut were ready to eat, and then she'd start new batches. When money ran low, she'd cook sauerkraut and kidney bean soup, thickened with flour.

Most of the time we kept our distance from the boarders. But William was still waiting for a chance to get even with Grizzly Bear.

One night, while Maureen and I were setting the table, William yanked Maureen's apron and grabbed a bowl as she ladled out soup.

"Let me help you tonight. I've done all my chores."

The two of them set out twenty-one bowls for the first shift, one by each chair. The boarders sat in the same spot for dinner each night, as if they had reservations. From upstairs, we heard boots pounding. The men were on their way down. Behind Maureen's back, William dumped half of the pepper shaker into Grizzly Bear's soup. He stirred it up with his finger. Then he pulled me with him into the sitting room.

"Just wait," he whispered in my ear.

We stood quiet as thieves in that room. From the dining room came the sound of chairs dragging as the men settled around the table.

"Take it easy!" complained one boarder. "You're hogging all the bread."

Ma passed around another loaf. "Here's more, boys. Eat up. How's the chicken soup?"

"Mrs. Chopp! This soups smells just like home." Grizzly Bear's voice boomed into the next room as he sniffed and slurped his soup at the same time. "It tastes— ah . . . ah . . . *Ah!Ah!Ah! CHOOOOOOO!*"

"*Hey!* Watch out!"

There was an uproar of voices. Chairs scraped against the floor.

"You sprayed us!"

"Your soup's all over my clean shirt!"

Then Grizzly Bear exploded. "What kind of soup are you serving, woman? It's too hot! My throat is burning."

"The soup is fine," a boarder scolded him. "You're the one making a mess!"

My mother's voice rose calmly and slowly above the fuss.

"Sit down, boys. I'll get some towels and clean you up in no time."

She ran so fast that we didn't have time to press our backs to the wall. She noticed us standing there but she didn't pause in her step. In a minute, she was back with towels and another bowl. She fussed and cooed over Grizzly Bear like a mother pigeon.

"Let me serve you a fresh bowl of soup," she coaxed him. "I hope you're not coming down with a flu. The soup will do you good."

The men started eating again. William motioned me to follow him outside. We hid in the backyard until the next shift was over and all the boarders had settled in the sitting room. Then we sneaked back inside and sat down at the table for dinner. William didn't dare look at Ma. She was in a stew, I could tell. Her foot tapped under the table and her lips were pressed in such a straight line, they looked like they'd been painted on.

William watched the clock, hoping the hours would pass so that he could go to bed. Ma waited until the chores and homework were done. At nine o'clock, she ordered him to his room. Phillip and I followed, hesitating in the doorway, but Ma motioned us to come in and close the door.

"There's too many people in this house for me to take care of. But I still got to raise you kids. It's my job to see you do right."

William swallowed so hard, his Adam's apple rode up and down his neck. Phillip, beside me, looked puzzled. He didn't know what was going on, but I did.

"Did you put pepper in that man's soup?" my mother demanded.

William nodded.

"Did your sister help you?"

My eyes popped. But William shook his head this time.

"You can't do that in this house!" She pointed her finger at him. "I run a business here."

She had been so quiet all evening, almost like a steel wire, but now her voice broke.

"You're growing up wild without a father. What would your pa do now if he were here?"

We all stood stiffly, facing Ma, arms flat at our sides like soldiers. Our eyes were riveted on her. She stared back at us, examining us like we were fresh-caught flies pinned beneath a microscope.

"Take off your belt, William," we heard her order.

He slipped it off and handed it to her with shaking fingers.

"Turn around. Pull your pants down. This is what my pa would have done to me. And this is what your pa would have done to you too, if he was around, bless his soul."

She whacked my brother ten times over his bottom, reddening his behind. Afterward, William stood up, rubbing the spot. He looked like a little boy and not the fresh-mouthed kid he usually was. His eyes were red too. It was the first time Ma had ever punished any of us.

My mother straightened up but didn't let go of the belt. All our eyes held on it.

"Next time you're in cahoots with your brother"—she eyed me and then Phillip—"either one of you, you'll get it too!"

She stormed out of the room. Phillip and I collapsed onto the bed. But William stood up, afraid to sit down, his mouth hanging wide open.

"I can't believe she did that," he complained.

"Ma's the boss of the boardinghouse," Phillip told im. "And she's the boss of us too."

Ma was our ma and our pa too. We had just forgotten. ut she never did.

Chapter 23
Reunion
Christmas 1927

Out of all the grayness of Schumacher leaped a brightness. At Christmas, Aunt Tracey and her family finally came to visit us as they had promised over a year before. We stood at the train station awaiting the Northland. I stepped away from the tracks, my back pressed against the station wall. Since that ride away from Cobalt, I never liked trains. But my brothers ran up and down the platform, yelling in the cold, sparkling air. Ma huddled in her black coat and looked into the distance.

The train roared in, shaking the ground beneath our feet. Everything flew into the air. Newspapers. Candy wrappers. I held tight to my hat and wiped my eyes clear of soot. That's when I saw my cousin Helen. She was the first one to jump off the train, bouncing like a kite in the wind.

"Where's Frances?" she screamed.

I stood, frozen, in my brother's old boots and patched jeans.

"Frances!" she called. "Is that you?"

She ran to me and twirled me around and around. From the top of my head to the tips of my fingers and down to my frozen toes, I began to warm up like it was summertime. I smiled for the first time since I'd moved to Schumacher.

Helen had arrived. She was nine years old, much taller than me, plump and blonde like her mother, with a round chest like a robin's breast. Ringlets jiggled like springs on her head. She wore a pink dress with gray woolen stockings and shiny dress boots. There was only one word to describe my cousin. Divine!

"We've been cooped up in that train all day. I walked from one end to another a hundred times, wobbling all the way. I felt like I was wearing high heels!" She balanced herself along the platform like she was standing on a tightrope.

By the time we reached the boardinghouse, I'd heard tons of stories about Cobalt. They filled me like bread. My aunt was heavier now, and Helen whispered to me right off that she was having a baby in the spring. Inside the house, the first thing Helen noticed was the stairway. Up she ran, but she stopped midway when she realized I wasn't following her. My feet were stuck on the bottom step where I had sat so often.

"Frances, aren't you coming up?" she called down to me.

I nodded but couldn't budge one foot. She skipped back down to me, reached out for a hand and together we walked up each step, one by one. I held on to the banister to steady myself. After an impossibly long time, I reached the top step, breathless. I had climbed a mountain of steps. The second floor stretched out in front of me, one door after another leading into darkened rooms. I raced ahead to them, holding Helen's hand. We peeked into the miners' empty bedrooms. Narrow cots were lined up in rows. White chamber pots waited beside them. I would never have dared step into those rooms by myself. But with my cousin beside me, I felt bolder.

That first day, when I reached the top of the stairs, I felt just like Helen. Until I had to go back down, that is. Then I turned into myself again. The steps led down just as steeply as they had gone up. It made me dizzy to look down. But Helen made a game of it. We both crawled down backward. My hands hugged each step the long way down.

By the end of the week, we were running up and down the stairs, pounding our shoes hard to imitate the miners' boots. We aimed spitballs straight into the spittoons. We kept on like that for days. She lifted me out of that gray place to a new place. From the moment I first set eyes on her again, she was all I thought about. My brothers seemed to disappear, and Ma too. If I shut my eyes, I could just see Helen's face, smiling back at me. Nobody seemed to mind what we did. Nobody told us what to do or not to do. They left us alone. Everybody was too busy. The house filled with a new sound.

Laughter.

In Cobalt, I'd heard laughter only a few times. It was a long time before I heard it at all and longer still until it was a part of our lives. My two brothers grinned all the time. They knew what a joke was, William especially. He was always up to something. Usually it was crude, like blowing farts into a jar. But Aunt Tracey was the first one I heard belly laugh. She laughed so hard, her face turned red. She could make anyone laugh. She got Ma going too. She's the only one who could. My mother laughed so much, tears rolled down her cheeks. Her blue eyes sparkled. Even in her black dress, she no longer looked gray.

The house changed too with the coming of my relatives. It no longer was the boarders' place. It belonged to us. Most of the boarders left for a few days. The mines were closed and anybody who had family in Canada or the United States left to visit them. It was the one holiday in the whole year when nobody worked. My aunt and her family filled the house up as they had our Cobalt cabin, making it a home.

Aunt Annie's Christmas letter arrived. None of us kids had met her, but we all wanted to. My mother's and Aunt Tracey's eyes lit up whenever they talked about their oldest sister. She had the farm everyone wanted and seven strong sons to run it. She seemed to live in a fairy-tale land, while we had only lived in cold mountain places.

Dear Sisters,

I always think of you. You live in the same country as me, the same province, but we haven't seen one another for ten long years. Your lives are hard: Matt in the Cobalt mines and Frances running the boarding-house.

My dream is that we could all be together, living so close by that on Sundays, we could visit the whole day.

You could eat all the food we make on this flat farm—peach pie from the orchards, smoked spareribs and fresh-picked corn that melts in your mouth. Your children could run around the acres with my boys.

I pray that someday you will visit me. If you do, I know you will want to stay.

Your loving sister,
Annie

At last the cousins had time to take us into the evergreen forest. We climbed up a steep mountainside in search of the perfect Christmas tree. It was my first time out there. It was so hushed I had to walk on tiptoe. In the middle of that forest, though it was winter and so cold that my fingers were numb and not an animal stirred, everything was alive. I felt once again that the trees were watching me.

We all wanted the spruce tree when we saw it. It was wide and bushy, about nine feet tall. When we brought it into the living room, it touched the ceiling. It spread its blue-green arms everywhere. We decorated it with popcorn and snowflakes cut out of newspaper and set presents beneath it. If I closed my eyes and breathed in its evergreen scent, I could see the mountaintop it had once lived upon and the bright sky above it.

We went to bed late and awoke late. No one stirred before dawn. As soon as I opened my eyes, my feet hit the floor, racing through the house to find my cousin. Even before breakfast, she chatted up a storm about dresses, hair ribbons and boys. She ran from one thing to another: knitting a long red scarf, exploring the basement, sledding down the hill at the end of the street. She was interested in everything. Best of all, she pulled me along, a dark-headed twig of a girl. It suddenly seemed I was no longer four, but nine years old, just like Helen.

In the afternoons, we were a house of women. Ma and Aunt Tracey talked while Helen and I played. The men went ice fishing and took the boys with them. It didn't matter how raw the wind blew, they still went. Uncle Matt had grown up ice fishing in Calumet. In the fall, he said, the fish dived down deep, feeding off the bottom, keeping still. But come winter, they grew restless. They would jump at anything.

There weren't any worms to be dug then. They were hibernating. My uncle baited with dried corn, softened enough to slip on a hook. Yellow-eye, he called it, for the fish spy it shining like gold in the dark waters and nibble for it. He baited with sausage too, smoky and salty. Come-and-get-it, they called that bait, for they swore the fish smelled it and dashed up to the surface for it. They brought home pails of pickerel and pike. My aunt fried the fish in flour with a hint of garlic. We ate it steaming hot with homemade french fries and corn fritters. You didn't hear anything out of us except "Mmmm!"

But the holiday was soon over. The boarders came back, one by one. Our relatives had to return to Cobalt. Once again, we stood on the platform awaiting the Northland. Ma looked small in her coat beside Aunt Tracey, plump and loud voiced. My aunt seemed bigger to me than all of Schumacher. I wanted to tug on her coat to stay. Tears must have flooded my eyes, for Helen put a finger to her lips.

"Don't cry. We'll see you soon."

We hugged tight and then she was gone. My mother leaned toward the track, her shoulders hunched. We all stood waving after them, wishing we were aboard that train on its way back to Cobalt, but none of us dared say that aloud.

Chapter 24
Isolation
March 1928

A letter fell through the mail slot. I ran to Ma with it right away. That night, she read the news to all of us as we sat around the dining room table.

Dear Frances,

Matt was hurt in a rockfall in the shafts. His chest was crushed and his leg was broken. Today, he is coughing blood and has a high fever. The doctor said he has a collapsed lung. In the midst of it all, my baby Margaret was born. She seems frail.

My neighbor says her husband broke his hip in the fall, and as he is old, he will never work again. Old Mrs. Janeck lost her son that day. He leaves ten kids at home.

Paul wants to get a job at the mines but I won't let him go.

We are all worried. In Matt's fever, he did not know who we were.

Missing you all,
Your loving sister,
Tracey

There was silence around the table. Everyone stopped eating. The words felt like carving knives sliced into our hearts.

"Will Uncle Matt live?" wondered Phillip.

Ma shrugged and looked into Joseph's eyes.

"When will we visit them again?" I asked. I wanted to catch hold of Helen's hand immediately and see for myself that she was all right.

Ma didn't answer. She had not spoken since she'd read the letter. Something made me walk toward her. As I got close to her, I saw the shininess in her eyes. She grabbed my shoulder and pressed her head hard to my chest. Bitter tears fell onto my blouse.

"Those cursed mines!" She beat her fist on her lap. "I know just how Tracey feels."

My brothers exchanged guilty looks. Like our cousin Paul, they had wanted to go down into the Cobalt mines to see what it was like as soon as they were old enough.

Ma sat up in her chair, wiping her face dry.

"Get writing paper and a pen," she ordered Phillip. "Write down what I say. I'm not steady enough to do it myself."

Dear Tracey,

We are praying for Matt's recuperation. He is a big, strong man who loves everything about life. He will be up and around in no time.

How I wish we were together so we could lighten each other's loads. I am wiring you something. Please accept it as a gift to tide you over until Matt can return to work. You have a new baby to care for now. You have always watched over me, but now it's your younger sister's turn to help out.

Thinking of you all,
Frances, Phillip, William & Baby

The next day, Ma wired money to Cobalt. She had been saving it to spend on our Easter outfits. She asked us first if we would mind. Without a second thought, we all shook our heads. It was our cousins, Aunt Tracey and Uncle Matt that we missed.

I carried Raggedy Ann everywhere that week—into the kitchen, propped up beside me at dinner. I needed her eyes upon me. She steadied me. She was sewn together with pieces of everyone. Maybe she could make things whole.

On Palm Sunday, our family went to church with the cousins. Ma asked the priest to say the mass especially for Uncle Matt. She stayed on her knees during the whole long mass with her head bent, wrapped in her black mourning coat. Our movements in the wooden pews echoed up into the high ceiling. Incense smoked the air. Latin words rang like gongs in our heads. They seemed to toll out the word *death, death, death* into our open ears. I sang as loud as I could to block out that sound.

On Good Friday, a telegram was delivered to our door. Ma held it in her hands, trembling. We all gathered around her. We were dressed in our good clothes, ready for church.

"I can't read it." She handed it to my older brother.

He scanned his eyes across the thin page.

Matt's fever is gone. He has pain but knows us all.
Thank you for your prayers. Tracey.

My mother leaned against the wall while my brothers whooped it up and ran like wild men up and down the hallway. In church that afternoon, Ma's face drooped but she was smiling. Our prayers had been answered.

Easter Sunday was quiet. Some boarders stayed on, and the cousins, of course. Peter was off visiting a Croatian maid he had met in town. But Joe seemed different. He didn't even look up to yell at us while we tore through the house searching for colored eggs. He sat slumped in the living room, his long legs stretched out. Every once in a while, he pulled a letter out and read it, shook his head and stuffed it back into his pocket. He spent hours in his chair. He spoke to our mother in Croatian, with long drawn-out words, heavy as rocks in his mouth.

"He got a letter from Severin," Ma told us.

We knew that back home, Joe had a wife named Vinka and a daughter, Novenka, William's age. We'd seen a picture of the two of them, both unsmiling. Vinka wore a bandanna over her head and hooped gold earrings like a gypsy, and Novenka shrank away from the camera.

"What did Vinka say?" William asked.

Ma sighed. "She asks if Joe has forgotten her. It's been three years since he left. Novenka doesn't remember her own pa. She asks Vinka when she will see him, but she has no answer for her."

"They could just come over here like Joe did," said Phillip.

"Joe wants to buy a farm first like Aunt Annie. He sends money back home and saves every penny he can, but it's not enough yet."

"When will it be enough?"

"Not for years yet." Ma frowned. "But Vinka can't wait."

William had an idea.

"They could come and stay with us."

"Takes time to arrange papers, son. Even if Joe fills them out now, it'll be a year before we see them here."

Croatia was a distant place.

Chapter 25
A Flurry of Letters
Spring 1928

I began to see my cousin Novenka's face clearly in my mind. Her sepia-colored photograph sat on Joe's dresser, and I sneaked a peek at it during the day while he was at work. She was a flat, tall girl like her father, with bony shoulders and cheekbones. Her eyes were the color of polished wood, and they popped out of her thin face. She had a hungry look, like she was empty. I began to speak to her.

"If only you could come here," I told her, "and eat Ma's mashed potatoes with cream and butter and kielbasa, you'd feel better."

I sat around the table and listened closely to stories about the old country. Novenka and her mother lived on an old farm with too many relatives and never enough food. The money Joe sent was split among twenty people. There wasn't a penny left over. Vinka and my cousin spent their days wandering through the woods with buckets and a knife. They gathered fallen logs and dragged them home for the woodstove; picked dandelion greens and mushrooms for dinner; and checked traps for rabbits and pheasants. In her picture, Vinka, with wide shoulders and big hands, stood as tall as Joe. She wore rubber boots and faded overalls like she was ready to work in the fields.

One night after dinner, while the adults sipped coffee, Joe announced, "I've heard from immigration. Canada will let my family come over."

We all stared at Joe. He had filed papers long before Vinka's Easter letter and never told anybody, not even her. It took many months to get such news.

"Novenka?" The word popped out of my mouth.

"And Vinka too. I'd like to bring over more of her family, but I can't afford it."

"When do you think we'll see them?" asked Ma.

"By the year's end. I had hoped to be settled in a better place by then, but I can't wait any longer."

"They'll be fine here. Vinka's strong. She'll help me run the boardinghouse. We won't need outside help."

Joe smiled at my mother. Everyone, including my brothers and me, raised our cups of milk to him.

"Congratulations!"

All I thought about was Novenka. She didn't seem like a stranger. She dressed in hand-me-downs like me. I could teach her English, and I'd have her company every day. It would be like having a sister. I remembered what it was like when Helen visited at Christmas and how she had shaken the grayness out of the days. I could barely fall asleep most nights, waiting for her to come.

But then the letter arrived from Cobalt. Ma's lips turned down when she read it. Uncle Matt couldn't walk after the fall. His back had collapsed. Most of the time, he lay flat in bed. The doctor said he wouldn't be able to return to the mines for a year. The family received no allowance from the mines to live on. The new baby was not gaining weight, and Paul had disappeared one morning. He had taken a job at the mines, in spite of his mother's pleadings.

"They're in a bind," Joe said. "It doesn't pay for them to stay on there. They should leave."

That's when the flurry of letters began, back and forth, between Ma and Aunt Tracey, between Aunt Elsie and Ma. All her sisters wrote and worried about Matt and Paul, at thirteen too young to work in the mines. Vinka wrote too, with questions about her papers and what to bring to America.

In the midst of it all arrived Aunt Annie's letter. It was so clear, it was almost as if she were standing in the room beside us, a wide-hipped, gray-haired woman, wearing an apron, ready to ask us to sit down and serve us tea and pound cake, as we heard they did in gentle Canadian homes.

Dear Sister and family,

You have all had enough up north. Loss, sorrow, endless work. It is a tough country up there. I know because we gave it ten years. Those were the hardest years of our lives. Even though I work every second on this farm, my work here is happiness.

I believe our sorrows will lessen if we are all together—Tracey, Matt, their kids, Frances and her kids, Joe, Vinka, Novenka and the Slivacs. Family should be together. That's what our mother would have wanted, bless her soul.

I found a house for rent in Hamilton, fifteen miles from Simcoe. It's big and cheap, near the steel mill, where they are hiring men right now. Men are safer there than in any mine.

Think it over.

Annie

It was as if a warm wind had swept through the deep freeze of Schumacher, melting the ice in my mother's heart.

"If it could only be true!"

"I'd go in a minute," Joe told her.

"Me too!" Mike said. "I've had enough of this place."

He poked his brother in the ribs. Peter finally nodded too.

We all looked at Ma.

"But how can I live there?" she asked. "If you men get jobs, how will I make money?"

"We'll start another boardinghouse," offered Joe. "Buy a big house. We'll have enough money if we both split the cost."

My mother wrote to Aunt Tracey that very night but never told us what she said. She wouldn't dictate it but sat up late at the kitchen table, writing it, her head right next to the paper. She had received new glasses less than a year before, and already she squinted.

At certain times during the next weeks, I'd watch her pace between her chores, instead of sitting down. Her mouth was flat and her arms were folded tightly against her chest. Around the rooms she moved, her busy hands not dusting or straightening things as they usually did, her boots clicking against the linoleum, her black woolen skirts heavy as old drapes swooshing.

"Ma's on pins and needles, waiting for Aunt Tracey's letter," Phillip warned me. "Don't go near her."

No one had to tell me that. When Ma got like that, even Joe knew to leave her alone.

The letter finally came from Aunt Tracey. Ma tore it open and frowned. She grabbed her coat and stormed off to town to send a telegram to our aunt. She stomped back through heavy snow, inches of it piled on her shoulders. She didn't say a word to us, just went back to her cooking pot.

Three weeks later, we received an answer.

Dear Sister,
You are somebody to reckon with. We cannot say no. Matt has finally agreed. He was very stubborn. He's just like you. We will go to Hamilton in June to stay with you. Paul will get a job so we won't be broke.

Thanking you,
Your loving sister,
Tracey

Ma had decided to take Aunt Annie's offer, and that meant everyone else had to come too. That was Ma's way. There would be room for all of us in Hamilton and some boarders too. But the boarders would be guests, my mother promised, who would tiptoe around us. Best of all, I would not be surrounded by men. Helen and Novenka would come, the sisters I'd always wanted, and baby Margaret too.

When the snows ended and new green was popping out of those forever brown trees, we were ready to leave Schumacher. Ma had whatever was left of the settlement money in a pouch inside her suitcase, together with money from the sale of the Cobalt cabin. She never let that suit-case out of her sight.

The Slivac brothers and Joe went ahead of us to get jobs at the steel mill. We said good-bye to all the boarders, even Grizzly Bear. Only Goldilocks looked sad, his beard drooping. A new woman took over the boarding-house. She waved her rolling pin in the air as a good-bye.

"Good riddance!" Ma mumbled under her breath to the boardinghouse, but we all heard her and laughed.

This time, no one turned back to look at Schumacher. My whole family faced south. My brothers raced ahead through the moving cars all the way to the head car, eager to get to Hamilton faster than anyone. I sat still with Raggedy Ann on my lap. She flopped against me, so soft with wear, she felt like a pillow. I nestled beside my mother. She sat quietly, breathing in and out, her head leaning back on the cushion. Her lips were open. I believe she was smiling.

Hamilton,
Southern Ontario

You changed my mourning into dancing;
You took off my sackcloth and clothed me
With gladness.

—Psalm 29 (30)

Chapter 26
The House on Bigger Avenue
Spring 1928

From far off, we saw the smoke. We stuck our heads out the window as the train neared the big city. Steam brewed up in clouds like a million teakettles boiling over. There was a smell of something burning in the air. It was the steel company, Ma said, belching smoke everywhere. Behind it was a patch of blue-gray. Lake Ontario. Boats sailed across it, carrying goods from Toronto. Steamers drifted by, full of sightseers. Stretching along the lake was a low ridge, an escarpment, spreading long miles off into the distance. We wanted to see everything all at once. We were itching to get off that train after our two-day ride.

In downtown Hamilton, Joe met us at the station with Aunt Annie's husband. Uncle Jack was over six feet tall with a full head of red hair. He wore suspenders to hold up his baggy jeans. As we stood talking in the street, he motioned us to move off the road. Waves of steamy heat shimmered off its black surface. Our shoes sizzled. An odor hung in the air like damp wood left smoldering too long.

"That road is coated with tar block," he warned. "On a hot day, that tar heats up so much, it'll stick to your shoes like gum."

A blast of hot wind hit our faces. I soon felt overheated in my boots and wool sweater. My whole body steamed up like the road.

"It's already summer here!" Ma complained, yanking off my sweater.

"This ain't nothing yet," Uncle Jack joked. "It's about eighty degrees today and it's still spring. Wait till August."

"Sure isn't like up north," said Joe. "This is like standing in a furnace!"

"That's how it is when you live between a lake and an escarpment. All the heat gets trapped on this flat land." Uncle Jack laughed. "You could fry an egg on this street today. But it sure makes the corn grow."

We piled into his truck and left downtown, bumping along the streets, passing houses and factories. Finally, at a big cotton mill, we slowed down and turned the corner. At the end of the street was the house they had rented for us.

"Ten bucks a month is all they wanted for her," our uncle said, grinning.

It was a tiny cottage with windows only in the front. It looked as thirsty and tired as we did. It had once been painted green, but all that was left was a chip of it here and there. Mostly it was raw dry wood. Piles of old mattresses, plaster and iron bedposts were piled up in the backyard, remnants of the families who had once lived there. Not a blade of grass grew anywhere, just tall weeds. Burdock. Blue-flowered chicory. Plenty of dust. Across the street was a huge field filled with heaps of decaying food and old boxes. The town garbage dump.

"That's why the rent's so cheap," I heard my mother mutter.

Then we saw a blur of white on the stone porch of the cottage. A woman in an apron stepped out, wide hipped, with her gray hair in a neat bun. She moved as gracefully as a breeze and smiled wide when she saw us.

"You kids must be starving!" she called to us. "Such a long trip on a hot day. Come sit down at the table. Pour yourself a tall lemonade."

No one had to tell me who she was. It was Aunt Annie. She gathered us all in a big bear hug. She shooed my brothers to the table, but she gathered me close again.

"What a pretty girl you are! Skinny as a soup bone though. You just wait and you will find a place here. Not all at once. But, here and there, bit by bit, you'll see something to love in Hamilton like you did in Cobalt. It happened to me when I came here. It'll happen to you too."

I let her pat my brown hair smooth. She fit my whole skull into her palm as if it belonged there. She knew me by touch, as if her fingers recognized me, and I knew her the same way. She was how I had imagined her. I had traveled a long way to find her.

We stepped into the cottage. Inside, it was softly lit with kerosene lanterns. Our aunt had hung curtains, bought furniture and set a round oak table with dinner. The house smelled delicious. Sweet hot rolls. Kielbasa. Sauerkraut. Chicken soup. Baked potatoes. For dessert, Aunt Annie had baked a poppy seed pound cake. She cooked better than Ma did. We ate and ate.

I fell asleep sitting at the table that night, my head pressed into my mother's side while Ma and Aunt Annie talked endlessly. What I remember most is my aunt's voice. It rang clear and loud like a bell. It made me smile just to listen to it.

"Looks like a scared little thing," I heard Aunt Annie say that night. "Lost her pa and the only girl with two rough boys. I ought to know, with seven boys myself. No wonder she clings to you, Frances."

It was as if she put a finger on a wound that no one noticed. She knew me through and through, though I hardly spoke a word to her. I thought no one could guess my secrets.

Chapter 27
Squeezing In
Summer 1928

It was a skinny cottage with tiny rooms, but we squeezed ourselves in. Joe and the Slivacs slept in the dining room. We shared a room in the back. Aunt Tracey's family, when they came, would have the big bedroom. The two bedrooms upstairs were filled almost overnight with six boarders from the steel mill.

When the south wind blew, it carried the breath of the dump from across the street straight into our house. The stink of rot magnified by hot air. Flies clustered everywhere. Fly strips hung from the ceiling, waving like curtains. We awoke to endless buzzing in our faces. But that was not the worst of it. The rats were. They scurried all over the street at night, sliding out of the channels leading in from the lake. They sneaked under our house and squeezed up through the floorboards, sniffing for food. In the dark as we lay in bed, we could hear their claws scratching to get in. My brothers cut branches from willow trees and chased the rats all through the house, switching their tails with the willows, until they ran out. Once, a rat slid across Ma's foot as she was lifting a ten-gallon pot of soup. She got so scared, she spilled that soup all over the floor.

Finally, in June, our other relatives arrived. Ma said we had to squeeze in tight, like a sandwich, but none of us minded. It was like Christmas every day at first. We all seemed to fit together like we once had in Cobalt. My brothers had Paul to run with in the evenings. He got a job at the coal company. He lied about his age to get in. In no time at all, he looked older too. Black coal dust coated his skin and hands. Although he scrubbed with a brush in the backyard as his ma insisted, his fingers never came clean.

Helen and I were each other's shadow. I had a sister ready made in her. She loved to comb my hair and make me laugh. She teased my brothers until they chased her around the house. I would never dare do such a thing. Almost five years old, I was no longer the youngest in the family. There was baby Margaret to play with now. We were always passing her from hand to hand—like a slice of bread, Uncle Matt joked, for she was as light as that. My uncle and aunt had loved me since the day I was born. With them around, the new boardinghouse felt like home.

Our house kept pace with the neighborhood steel mill, where all the boarders and the cousins worked. Lunches were packed just before the whistle blew and set at the door for the men: thermoses of steaming black coffee, thick beef sandwiches, and pasties—salty pies baked with meat and potatoes. The table was set for the men even if they didn't return until eleven at night. Steel workers were always hungry when they came home. Ma was the only one still awake at midnight, washing dishes and raising dough for the next day's bread.

One morning, Ma and Aunt Tracey sat at the kitchen table in their nightgowns, drinking coffee and frowning. I thought they would be happy together. It was what my mother wanted, what we all wanted. But something was wrong. I listened close to see what the trouble was.

"We're at one another's elbows," my aunt complained, "with all the boarders and your kids and mine. We have to line up to go to the bathroom. Yesterday, Helen was late for mass, waiting to wash up."

Ma nodded and sipped her coffee.

"There's more I have to tell you." Aunt Tracey hesitated. "I think . . . I'm pregnant again."

Ma looked up. "You sure?"

"Pretty sure. We didn't plan on another one. Matt's doing odd jobs around the neighborhood, but he can't lift anything yet. Doctor's orders. If only he'd get better. Then he could work at the steel company."

"Times are tight, Tracey. Joe and I had planned to look around and buy a big house together. Maybe now's the time."

"Where will we get the money? None of us works, except Joe and my son. The boarders don't bring in enough for us to save."

"Never you mind," Ma said. "I got something stashed away."

"You mean the Cobalt money?" my aunt gasped.

"Yes. From the settlement. I saved most all of it."

"How did you get by without spending it? I thought it was long gone."

"Scrimping. Sewing my own clothes. And I did make money on that boardinghouse with Joe. He made some and I made some."

"Do you trust him?"

"He's our cousin. He stood by me when I needed him and got me out of Cobalt. I wouldn't have made money on the boarders without him."

"It'll take more than boarders to make money," my aunt said. "We'll have eight kids between us when Vinka comes. Where will we put everybody?"

Ma just sighed and nodded wearily.

Not a Sunday afternoon passed that we didn't want to go to the Simcoe farm. That was the only day farmers did not work. Simcoe was the opposite of Hamilton. It was not like any place I knew. Not like Schumacher. Not like my faraway memories of Cobalt, where wilderness closed you in with blue sky and pine trees. If I climbed up the hayloft to the very top of Uncle Jack's barn, I could stand at an open window and look out over the fields. From that spot, in all directions, I could see the farm I had dreamed about when Ma had read my aunt's letters aloud.

The fields stretched out over a hundred acres, my uncle said. Flat and tame, burned honey yellow by the sun. Hay fields. Wheat. Corn. Cool green grass around the house. The Victorian farmhouse gleaming so bright white on an August afternoon, it hurt my eyes to look at it.

On that farm, I made a friend for life. Lady was a plain

old black farm dog, huge as a pony. She herded sheep and bossed cows and kept Uncle Jack company. No one would have said she was pretty. No one would have thought of her as a pet either, except me. Farmers did not keep animals for pets, only for work. Most folks around thought she was mean. Lady guarded that farm like she owned it, sniffing along the perimeter of the fields for trespassers. She could snap a groundhog's neck in two. All the wild creatures hid when she prowled. But when she saw me, Lady ran right over and shoved her big head in my hand, demanding a stroke. She never left my side.

The farm was on a dirt road in the middle of nowhere. Once in a while, a car drove past. You could hear it coming a long way off, flinging stones in the road. Lady heard it first. She slunk down, creeping toward the road like a wolf. She disappeared through tunnels in the high grasses. If you knew where to look, you'd see just her pointy tail poking up. The instant the car drove by, that dog burst out like gunshot and leaped at the driver. We'd see the car swerve and almost land in a ditch, the driver got so frightened. Lady would chase it all the way down the road until we couldn't see it anymore. She always came back with her head held high.

In the middle of summer, when Hamilton was sizzling, you just had to sit on Aunt Annie's back porch, where the breezes blew in from all over the fields, cooling you. In that place, when the heat of the afternoon reached its peak, Aunt Annie appeared in a white cotton dress, her skirt billowing in the wind. She stood tall in the doorway, her hand shielding her eyes. She scanned the low clouds on the horizon, searching for signs of rain to drown the throats of the parched wheat. I looked out with her, across the fields, and remembered her promise to me when we first met: *You'll see something to love in Hamilton like you did in Cobalt. Here and there. Bit by bit.*

All the cousins, thirteen of us, sprawled out on the cool wooden boards of the porch, guarded by Lady, after all our running and playing was done and all the lemonade was drunk. Ninety in the shade, Uncle Jack boasted. Some on our backs, sleeping. William blowing tunes on a blade of grass held between his fingers. Helen humming along with him, stretched out beside me. Baby Margaret studying how the hazy clouds puffed up in the distance. Me lying on my belly, chin in hand, watching the fields, and how the hot wind folded down the tips of the wheat. Everything moved. Everything waved. The hay lilted. The summer corn reached straight to the sun. Even the orange daylilies in the flower beds leaped up to dust my chin with pollen.

My very self danced there on top of the wheat. As if I had lifted off the earth. Floating. Dreaming. Soaring. It was then I remembered Cobalt and how music played there when I was small. A whispering of pine. The diamond sun. The world a bowl that held me safe. It made me smile. I thought it was forever lost. But here it was, in these flat fields, singing. I had gone so far away and come back to it again.

In those few fleeting moments, I believed we would find a home.

Chapter 28
September Changes Everything
Fall 1928

We couldn't afford to move out of the cottage. Prices for houses were far too high. Joe's plans for a bigger boardinghouse run by Vinka and my mother evaporated. So many immigrants swarmed into the country that the government froze all applications. It would be another year before we saw Vinka, they wrote us. We were all sitting around the dining room table when my mother told us her decision.

"I got a job," she announced. "At the Ideal Laundry on Barton Street. Frances will start school come September. I'll work the night shift and be home by breakfast. At night, my kids will be safe here with you."

Aunt Tracey stared at her like she'd lost her mind.

"The night shift at a laundry? That's hard work!"

"Never mind. I've got to do it."

"How many days a week?" asked my uncle.

"Six," she muttered.

All the adults looked at her.

"I can't sit around here and take care of ten boarders. It doesn't bring in enough. Someone's got to go out to work."

"How much will they pay you, Ma?" asked Phillip.

"Fifteen cents an hour." She sighed. "But I can work through my lunch hour. Eat standing up. I'll just need a new pair of shoes to hold up my legs."

We looked down at her shoes, thin and cracked, the only pair she owned. My aunt just shook her head. But nobody fought Ma. They knew better than to argue with her. Someone had to make money. Joe, the Slivacs and Paul were the only workers. Aunt Tracey was with child and Uncle Matt was stooped over, always in pain. But why did Ma have to be the one to go?

September came. The morning I started school at St. Anne's, a half mile away on Barton Street, Ma kissed me good-bye.

"Don't look so glum, Baby. You're off to start a brand-new life of learning. You'll do fine. I'll wait for you to come home every day."

I squeezed my new notebook and pencil case tightly to my flat chest.

"Hurry up now. Go with your brothers. They'll show you the way."

Helen grabbed my hand and we both ran to catch up with them. Ma always said my brothers had the wind at their backs and they did. I dashed through the street behind them, tears at the corners of my eyes. I would have turned around and run back home to Ma if I hadn't heard Phillip challenging us, "Last one to school is a rotten egg!" That made Helen run faster, pulling me in her trail.

That day in school, I learned I had to sit tall, my back braced against a hard wooden chair, and keep my eyes on the teacher at all times. But my eyes kept straying to the other boys and girls in the straight rows around me. Thirty of us. Girls in one row. Boys in the next row. Most dressed in threadbare clothes and torn shoes. Some had uncombed hair and sleep still stuck in their eyes. But Ma had made me awaken early, scrubbed my skin shiny red and laid out my best dress.

The school was ruled by nuns. The principal, Sister Ciprian, pounded through the halls, frowning, a long red strap hanging from her belt. None of us kids ever spoke to her unless we were in trouble. My first-grade teacher was Sister Fabian. She was old, veiny faced and wide. She dressed in long black robes from head to toe. They swished as she walked the aisles, draping across our desks on both sides as she moved, touching us with their blackness. I stopped breathing when she came close. Her breath stank like sardines. Her eyes were razor sharp. They caught the littlest mistake or a back not held perfectly straight. She tapped her pointer at the spot and rapped the desk hard. Sometimes, she'd catch your knuckle and hit it too. But she never caught mine. I sat perfectly still in my best dress and listened close.

For all the first days, she went on and on about the alphabet. I didn't know what she was talking about. She tapped with her pointer to dark marks written on the wall above the blackboard. She made a big fuss about them. I stared there like she wanted but I still didn't understand. It was like she was speaking another language. But I didn't let on. I never raised my hand to ask a question. I just kept my eyes on her.

On the way home, Helen chatted endlessly about the boys in her fifth-grade class and the new uniform we were expected to wear by the next day. She never mentioned the alphabet, so I thought maybe it wasn't as important as Sister Fabian let on.

That night, Ma left for work. But first, she lay down with me, coaxing me to sleep. It was just past dusk and the birds were chirping quietly. Darkness fell. Ma slept. I watched her as if I would never ever see her again. I studied how she lay, her mouth slightly open, her body stiff like she was about to bolt up any moment. At ten-thirty, my aunt tapped on the door and called Ma's name. She jerked up and put on her heavy new shoes. She kissed me good-bye and clomped out of the room.

All that night, there was an empty spot beside me. No stars could be seen in the Hamilton sky. Soot and smoke hung in the air, blocking out their light. I remembered the nights in Schumacher, waiting for Ma. The million questions on my lips, unanswered. The nights here while she fed the boarders returning from the evening shift. I was always waiting for her. Finally, she'd come, and I would sink down into my blankets and dream. But no matter how long I waited now, it did not matter. Ma would not come back that night. She'd never lie beside me again, filling the space between me and the darkness, standing guard between me and it. She'd never make a safe, warm place for us again.

I started to cry. The tears kept coming, as if they'd been lined up, waiting to pour out. I stretched my head up to see if my brothers were sleeping across the room, but they did not stir. I thought of Novenka, staring so long at Canada with her eyes of polished wood that had lost all their shine. I buried my head in Raggedy Ann's mop and slept in fits.

Before long, it was dawn. My relatives stirred in the house. I heard my aunt calling us kids for our turn to wash up and come down to breakfast. Ma walked through the front door. She sat straight down and took off her shoes. Her shoulders sagged.

"Your feet are all swollen up," chided my aunt. "Here. Take a load off. Put them on this chair."

Ma sank back into the chair, removed her thick leggings and propped her feet up. My uncle placed a cup of steaming coffee in her hands. She closed her eyes and sipped it, sighing.

I gulped my breakfast and did not say a word. I kept my head down. When I had looked into the mirror that morning, my eyes were two slits, all bloodshot. I didn't want my mother to see. It would worry her. When it was time to leave, I kissed her on the cheek. I tried to smile, but instead I just swallowed hard. Ma smoothed down the collar of my white blouse and pressed the pleats of my navy skirt flat with her hands. It was the new school outfit everyone had to wear at St. Anne's.

"I'll bring your uniform to the laundry with me from

now on, Baby. Press it myself. You'll be the neatest girl in first grade."

For a brief moment, listening to her voice, the long night seemed to vanish. But then I remembered the coming night would be just the same. And all the weeknights forever ahead. I had the whole long day to face without her besides. Ma touched the corners of my mouth, tempting me to smile. And I did. Just for her. But the tears welled right up behind my throat. I ran out the door to get to school as fast as I could.

Chapter 29
St. Anne's
December 1928

Winters in Hamilton were endless gray, the clouds pressing low down over the lake, darkening the days. The air was always damp. No matter how many layers of sweaters I piled on, I always felt chilled. The only time it was pure white with light like Cobalt was when the snow first fell. But by the next day, it was brown with soot, melting into slush.

At times a sadness like a numbness fell over me. If anyone asked me what was wrong, I could not have said. I had too many feelings to put into words. I was afraid that they would all swarm out of me like a nest of angry, buzzing bees. There was no way to show it on my face. I wore a flat dull sameness, my lips in a straight line. It was how I looked as I went about my day.

Everything about me was brown. Skin darkened by the sun. Brown hair cut by Ma straight around with bangs. Brown eyes like a doe. I took to biting my lips in the evenings before Ma went off to work, dusky circles under my eyes. No one seemed to notice.

At home, I was invisible.

Summer and winter, I kept my eyes on the ground as I walked. I could have told you every weed that burst out of the side of the road. Where the chamomile grew and when it was ready to pick for tea. And about the great chicory plant reaching out its arms, topped with blue flowers like stars. But I couldn't have told you much about the sky. I didn't see it.

There was a web of loss around me that grew thicker as I grew taller. With each birthday came the memory of birth and death, side by side. Around the table as my family cut my birthday cake each year, I saw the faraway eyes of my aunt and uncle and mother, remembering. I heard the sighs of everyone.

Ma and I lived in two different places. She became a night owl, sleepwalking through the day. She worked beside my aunt, tight lipped, a blank expression on her face, inviting no conversation. Just when we could have talked, those few hours at dusk, she collapsed beside me in a silent heap.

I kept awake, watching her. She did not rest, even in sleep. She never stretched out her whole body in bed but slept in a ball, ready to bounce out at ten-thirty. I could see in her squeezed-up face and tightened fists that she was already working at the Ideal Laundry. It was a place where they washed, starched and ironed uniforms. All night long, she starched shirts, dipping them in barrels of white foam until her hands peeled. Then she switched to the mangle, a heavy machine that pressed uniforms between rollers. She stood the whole while, eating a cold roll and drinking coffee from a thermos, never taking a second off, for the boss watched who came and went and clocked every movement.

In the mornings, I dressed in starched clothes fresh from the Ideal Laundry. In my stiff uniform, the shirt bleached to snow whiteness and the skirt with its pleats so tight it reminded me of an accordion, I looked picture-perfect. My hair was combed flat with a satin bow on the side. My shoes were polished so shiny, William joked that they could outshine a brand-new car. In that outfit, I began for the first time to look out at the world around me. I had never really noticed it before.

My classroom was the only place I went alone, with no mother or cousin or brother in the seat next to me. I remember watching Helen disappear down the long hall-way that first day with all the taller boys and girls and how I had wanted to run after her. The school swallowed her up and I was suddenly left on my own. But, bit by bit, I became a part of things.

I remember when all this came about. It happened in a day.

Sister Fabian pointed to the letters and again we said them aloud.

"A-B-C, Dee, E-F-G!"

Our first-grade class sang them in a kind of tune that went up and down, repeating what she said. Sister Fabian loved to sing. She sang the morning hymns in soprano, loud and high, above all our blended voices. She sang about the Blessed Virgin and the Holy Ghost and now she was singing the alphabet too. What a strange thing to do, I thought. Then she borrowed letters from the alphabet chart and wrote them, scraping her chalk on the slate board, like you could just take any ones you wanted for free.

"C . . . a . . . t."

She held up a picture and asked someone in the class to tell her what it was.

Cat! The word leaped in my brain. I looked at the picture and then back at the letters that marched across the top of the blackboard. My eyes popped out of my head.

"C-a-t. Now you say it, class."

"C-a-t," we repeated.

Beside me, Brian was kicking Billy under his desk. Sally squirmed like she had to go to the bathroom and Bobby swatted a fly. But my eyes were riveted on the board. Sister Fabian copied more letters from the alphabet. What was she up to now?

"B-a-t."

This time she showed us a picture of a scary bat flying.

"*Bat!*" we cried out.

I could hardly stay in my seat. I wanted to touch the letters and grab them into my fists, down from the alphabet.

"These are families of letters," our teacher explained. "The letters make words and the words are language."

I couldn't believe it. It was the greatest thing that had ever happened to me. I lived in a house where I heard Polish, Croatian, German and Italian. I couldn't tell what anybody was saying. I studied faces and listened to voices to understand what someone meant, always guessing at their words, never knowing. Phillip called our house the Tower of Babel because so many different languages were spoken in it. We kids all spoke English. Only if we got in trouble would we hear about it in Croatian. But here was this nun telling me exactly what English was, that it could be written down to make words. English made sense. It sounded sweet, not garbled or harsh, like the boarders' languages. It had power.

From that day on, I held Sister Fabian in my gaze, as if she had turned into a monarch butterfly. She had changed everything with those letters. All I wanted was to hear more. With enough words, I could learn to read, she promised. I wanted the words to be mine. I wanted them to roll off my lips as they did from Sister Fabian's lips, firm and loud, naming things, owning them. I wanted to sing them and write them in straight letters across the blue lines of my notebook. Make sentences and tell stories with them. Make the words mine. Find a way to give voice to all the hidden things inside me. I knew then why the past was always a mystery. I had no words then. You need words to name things.

No one knew this but me. I kept it a secret. It swirled in the place where my voice had been on hold, silently waiting.

I swallowed the words whole.

Chapter 30
The Great Depression
November 1929

There was a flurry of movement in the streets. Shadows drifting past. Murmuring on every corner. Families with all their belongings packed up on porches. The next thing I knew, neighbors disappeared, never to return. People I was used to seeing every day vanished. Though they had once put money down in the bank to buy their house, Ma said, they had no more money left for the payments. Families left behind empty houses, the windows dark at night, staring out like gaping holes. Big notices were nailed on their doors, announcing the property now belonged to the bank.

Uncle Matt said he'd seen a ghost town up north and that's how it looked. A place where folks once lived and suddenly something happened to dry it all up. That something in 1929 was the stock market crash. Just putting bread on the table was the most anyone could afford. A friend from Cobalt wrote that the miners had abandoned the town. Nobody needed silver. I shuddered to think how empty Cobalt must be.

"I heard folks in New York City just leaped out their

office windows," Joe said. "They lost all their money. Not a cent left."

Ma called it another word, the Great Depression, like it was a mood that had settled on the country. Many people were homeless and many were sad. All around us in those abandoned houses, families sneaked in like thieves, their belongings tied up in rags and carried on poles. They slept a night or two in the empty houses, peering out the bare windows like they were haunting the place. You never noticed them leave. They slipped away at night. Some boarded empty railcars on the TH&B or CNR. Others just walked on. The rail yards were filled with hobos.

"Gypsies," Ma said. "Don't have a nickel to spend. Looking for food and work. Not finding it. Moving on again."

"Where do they go, Ma?" I wanted to know.

"Everywhere. The cities. The mines. But every place is as bad as here."

The Slivacs moved on too. Peter married the girl from Schumacher. He and his new wife went up to Timmins with his brother Mike to work the mines again. They hated living in a city, they said. They needed space and trees around them.

But Ma said we were lucky. Though we had to work hard, we had food on the table and a roof over our heads. We were lucky in another way too. There was no more money left in the banks. But my mother had not saved her money in the bank since leaving Cobalt or bought any stocks and neither had anyone else in our family. You had to have lots of money to do that, they thought. So she and Joe kept their money in suitcases under the bed. They thought it was safe there. They were just about the only folks during the Depression who had a nest egg.

Once a family crept into the empty house next door. They had been on the road for months, they said. They were thin, worn and raggedy. The small boy coughed a lot. They had no pa. He had left to find work and was supposed to send money but he didn't. They were forced to move on and now they had no place for him to get in touch with them. They lost all track of him. When Ma brought food to them, she knocked on the door but they would not answer, fearing it was the bank. By nightfall, the food was gone. Sometimes, the mother would pass by our house, wrapped up in many layers of clothes, a wool scarf covering her head. She nodded at Ma with darkly circled eyes. She looked like she could barely walk down the street.

There were no more jobs at the mill. Uncle Matt tried to get a job there but they wouldn't hire anybody. Workers were laid off, but not Joe, Paul or Ma. They talked all the time now about how the prices for everything, including houses, were falling. Maybe they'd be able to finally afford a house. Joe wrote to immigration but never seemed to receive an answer. I worried about Novenka, waiting at a broken-down farm in the old country, growing bony and angular like her mother.

At night after Ma left, I lay in bed, tossing and turning. The only ones awake in the whole house were me and baby Elizabeth, born last spring. Her cries and my aunt's footsteps running to feed her filled the night. I tried to close my eyes and sleep. I told myself I wasn't alone. Ma would be home in the morning. My uncle would save me if anything happened. My brothers were there too.

It didn't work. My mind was lit up. I seemed to be all alone. During the day, my brothers were off and running like racehorses. I couldn't keep up with them. They had their own friends now. On hot days, you'd find them huddled over a game of dice in the shady backyard. Come winter, when the lake froze over, they grabbed sticks for ice hockey and sledded to the lake a mile off, without me.

I spent my days and my thoughts by myself. I had no friends my own age. I tagged behind Helen whenever I could. In the afternoons, I babysat Margaret and Elizabeth while my aunt cooked. They were both lively and never stopped talking. The house of girls, Uncle Matt called us now. My two baby cousins trailed me like I had all the answers to their constant questions. I noticed how easily they smiled and how bright their eyes were each morning as soon as they awoke, shaking their curly blond heads. They were not born in shadow, as I was.

One winter's night, while I was lying in bed, I heard a forlorn, high-pitched cry. It called again and again outside my open window. Maybe it was a lost child, one of the gypsy folk, not knowing which house its family slept in that night. I grabbed cheese from the kitchen and ran out. Snowflakes swirled wildly around me.

A dark form crouched behind the fence.

"C'mon out of there," I coaxed. "I have something for you."

It stood absolutely still. A black kitten trembled all by itself. Scrawny, thin boned, with matted fur, its ears up but its tail down. If I moved closer, it stepped back. If I stood my ground, it stood its ground. So I put the food down and tiptoed inside to watch from my window. The kitten crawled across the frozen yard and gobbled that food down.

Each night, it came back. I was ready with more food. Sometimes, I heated up milk. It loved that the best. It began to bring others with it, more kittens, brothers and sisters perhaps, and a mother too. Even cats had been made homeless by the Depression. Soon, I was feeding a pack of twelve cats left by families who had had to run off without them. All motley. All scared. But by that time, they were running up to me, rubbing their backs against my legs, purring in cracked tunes. Their heads darted if there was a sound in the street. Some jumped up in the air like they were spooked, but they always rushed back to me. I had tamed them.

I never told anyone about them, not even Helen, to whom I whispered most everything. I kept them a secret, a little family I was feeding, like my mother fed the families who drifted by. I wished I could take them all in. But I knew if I even took one, Ma wouldn't allow it. We have enough mouths to feed, she would say, and no extra milk for cats. So I fed them this way, by the fence, in the dark, so that no one would know.

By the end of that winter, we got a telegram from immigration. Joe's family was coming and the government was sorry for the delay.

Vinka and Novenka sailed on a huge boat from Croatia to Canada. They landed in Toronto first and traveled by steamer to Hamilton. When Joe brought them in the house, they looked just like their photograph. Novenka was taller than me, for she was nine. But she had that same look on her face as she had for the camera. She shrank into herself, making herself small. She did not know one word of English. She was dressed in farmer's clothes, boy's clothes, hand-me-downs like I used to wear up north. Vinka, beside her, so tall, seemed like a man with broad shoulders and big hands. Her voice in Croatian was loud as if she were calling from a barn. She grabbed my mother and hugged her hard. They both cried.

But Novenka stayed put behind her mother, squeezing her hands tightly together. In the midst of all the talking, I walked over to her. Somehow I felt older than her although I was only six. I knew what it was like to be yanked from the home you loved best.

I reached out for my cousin's hand. It was cold and stiff.

"*Dobar dan!*" I welcomed her.

She studied me for a few minutes. A tiny smile began to peek across her face, making her look like a little girl. Her hand soon felt soft as dough in mine. She began to melt in front of me like one of my stray cats.

Chapter 31
Brightside

1930

Ma and Joe bought a big boardinghouse together at Number 2 Birmingham Street, a mile and a half from the cottage. The owners had abandoned it. Ma and Joe bought that house outright from the bank for eight hundred dollars flat, four hundred each. It was a bargain. A gray-shingled house with ten bedrooms upstairs and three downstairs.

The neighborhood was called Brightside, but I had no idea why at first. There wasn't anything bright about it. Perhaps the English who first settled it hoped there would be.

When we arrived, the stink of burning metals hit our noses right off. The wind was gusting in from the lake. It tossed flat specks up into the air, gray as soot but hard as flint. They dusted the shoulders of Ma's black suit. Uncle Jack said it was ash from the metals burning in the steel factory.

"They're firing up that blasted furnace right now." Uncle Jack checked his watch. It was six P.M. "Every six hours, they load up the furnace with iron ore and it flares up high."

He pointed to the chimney of the steel mill. It towered hundreds of feet above the bedraggled houses. A flame burned day and night, summer and winter. It rose straight up, a red tongue leaping for air. If the fire went too low, he explained, it couldn't melt iron ore to make the steel. That fire had to be red-hot at all times.

My brothers seemed hypnotized by the flame, just two blocks away. They ran down the street toward it, Ma's calls drifting in the smoky air behind them.

"They can't go far, Frances," Uncle Jack said to calm Ma down. "There's only a few streets between here and the lake."

"They shouldn't go near the mill. It's dangerous!" she argued. "And they can't go near the lake without someone to watch them."

"The kids'll be all right," our uncle promised. "I'll trail behind them."

I tore after my brothers. By the time Uncle Jack caught up, all three of us were standing at the bottom of the mill looking up. My brothers pointed to a blast of red-and-gold-sparkled air that shot out of the chimney like fireworks. Phillip's hair was covered with gray dust. He looked like an old man. Around us, workers scurried in and out of the factory like ants, carting iron ore in bins from the rail yard.

"There's something a lot prettier than that old fire." Uncle Jack pointed to a gleam of blue like a shining eye beyond the factory.

In the same instant we saw it, all three of us took off

running again, past the workmen and the piles of steel, across the railroad tracks, right to the end of the land.

"On a clear day, you can see across Lake Ontario all the way to Toronto, some forty miles off. Not that we get too many blue days."

Ahead, water stretched out on all sides of us. Cobalt blue water. Waves slapping loudly against the gray sand. No beginning or end to the blueness. It seemed impossible for anything to be that big.

"Got any fish in it?" William asked.

"Smelts. Pike and perch too. You can fish all winter through the ice, just like up north."

Both my brothers had enough of just looking at the lake.

"Race you in!" yelled William. "Last one in is a rotten egg."

They flung their clothes off, stripped down to their underwear and stepped pale-skinned into the lake. My younger brother splashed past Phillip and dived in head-first. Phillip raced in after him. I heard them whooping and hollering, their screeches mixing with the cries of the great white seagulls circling above our heads.

"You jumping in, Baby?" coaxed my uncle. "I'll watch out for you."

I took off my winter boots and wool socks and tiptoed to the water's edge. The shore was rocky and sharp edges of stone cut into my bare feet. The ice-cold spring water shocked my skin. I let it touch me all the way up to my calves before the waves came in, threatening to drown me.

I stepped back. I stood on the shoreline, shivering, watching my brothers far off, wishing I wasn't six but twelve like Phillip, flinging my clothes off and doing what I pleased.

Uncle Jack plopped down on the sand and smoked a cigarette, laughing at my brothers. They finally came in, goose bumps on their white chests and arms, shaking themselves off like dogs.

"You're going to catch it from Ma!" I said.

"It'll be worth it," answered William. "Come morning, I'm running back with my fishing pole."

On the front porch of the new house, the relatives and boarders who moved with us stood around and talked. My two baby cousins climbed up and down the front steps, their faces flushed. The men smoked in a huddle, apart from the women. They were all congratulating Uncle Matt, who had just gotten a job at the steel company.

But Ma was waiting for us on the sidewalk, both hands on her hips.

"Where were you?" she demanded.

My brothers stood sheepishly, their hair dripping wet. Ma looked at them like she'd like to give them a licking.

"They just went for a lark. Dipped into the lake. Boys will be boys," said Uncle Jack. All the men on the porch laughed.

The words poured out all at once from the three of us, about the lake and the fish. Ma ordered my brothers inside at once to change, looked me over, felt my legs and told me to change too.

The lake was the shining part of Brightside. I knew then why the old English settlers called it that. They must have named it for Lake Ontario, tossing in the bright sun all year long. The English came from an island surrounded by water. On Lake Ontario's shore, they must have felt at home, looking out across the lake, pretending it was endless sea.

But all these years later, everyone lived in the shadow of the factories. Stelco. Dominion Foundry. Quaker City. Laidlaw. Westinghouse. Norton Grinding Wheels. All the men worked there. The factories were the neighborhood clock. When the whistle blew at the change of shift, we knew immediately what time it was. 7:00 A.M. 3:00 P.M. 11:00 P.M. Minutes before and afterward, the streets swelled with armies of workmen, scurrying home or to work, lunch pails in their hands. On the way to work, they rushed, breathless, with their heads straight up, looking at the chimney of the mill. But on the way back home, they eyed their work boots, dragging their feet, dressed in soot from head to toe.

The houses were crammed in so tight together that there was just a narrow alleyway between them. Folks built fences with driftwood they gathered from the lake, but it didn't keep anybody out and it didn't keep anybody in either. Day and night those alleyways streamed with kids playing stickball, housewives calling their children and men shooting dice. There was plenty of screaming and yelling. We called it gossip alley because it's where you first heard whose family was coming over from the old country, whose mother-in-law was mean, and whose son had played hooky that day.

Come summertime in those streets around the mill, folks said it was five degrees hotter than anywhere else in Hamilton. It was hot, hazy and humid. It stayed over ninety degrees day and night for weeks on end. A heat wave. At night, we'd lie in our upstairs bedroom, drenched in sweat, tossing under a thin cotton sheet.

The ground rumbled with the movement of freight trains. The CNR, the Canadian National Railway that roared across the whole country. The TH&B that stopped at Toronto, Hamilton and Buffalo. These trains carried goods to and from the mills. In the evenings, Ma would stop whatever she was doing to listen to their whistles. They predicted the weather. If the call was sharp and loud, the weather would be clear. But if the whistle wavered, dim and sad, calling through mist and fog, it meant rain the next day.

Whenever the north wind blew, we had to shut our windows because the wind carried fumes and soot from the mills our way. If we left our clothes hanging too long on the clothesline, we'd have to wash them all over again. I was the one whose job it was to bring them in at dinner-time, so I know. I forgot plenty in the beginning. The only part about laundry I liked was collecting all the dry white sheets from the line on a winter's day, gathering them in my arms for a whiff of their sweet cleanness.

Mornings, a fine dust flew in the air, gray at first, then black. Our windows were coated dark as coal. Soot drives folks mad. I remember Mrs. Chernezski, an old widow, sweeping the sidewalks each morning. She went around the whole square block. By the time she got back to where she started, the pavement was fairy-dusted with black specks. So she'd circle the block again with her broom like she was trapped in a maze. If I was outside playing hopscotch with my cousins, she'd pat my head and smile, revealing her big gold teeth. She spoke to us in Polish and we shrugged back at her. She never learned one word of English, not even hello.

That's how some of the old folks were, Ma said. By the time they moved to Canada from the old country, it was too late for them to change. Brightside was filled with widows like that, dressed in black from head to toe. They had trailed behind sons and daughters from small villages in Europe. In their minds, they still lived on the farm where they were born, wishing they could go back. They never belonged to Canada like we wanted to.

Chapter 32
Who I Was

1931

I was inseparable from my two older girl cousins. They were my best friends, although they were opposites. Helen was like a showgirl, dancing, talking, the center of attention. She was always ready to laugh and run off somewhere for an adventure. She had a beauty I could never hope to have. Her blondeness, her swirly dresses, her long legs and loud laughter drew people to her. They couldn't help liking her. I worshiped her.

From the very first moment I heard about Novenka, although she lived far away, I knew how she felt. She was lost like the stray cats. She needed me. No one else did. At first, she was so scared in a strange house, she couldn't sleep. I slipped Raggedy Ann into her arms at night. How she stared at that old doll. It was as if she could hardly wait to lie down with it and hear all the stories stored in its straw bones. I swear she knew all about my longing for Pa too without my saying a word. In the mornings, she always carried Raggedy Ann back to me with a shy smile.

I began to teach Novenka English. We all went to a new school now, Holy Rosary. I wore the same uniform, only now I needed one a few sizes bigger to cover my legs, forever growing. Novenka went too, but she didn't smile at all. It was a blur to her, a Tower of Babel, I suppose. She couldn't keep up with the kids her own age, so she was placed in my fourth-grade class. Novenka's eyes were always on me and never left my face, just as mine had studied Sister Fabian when I was in first grade. Listening. Learning. She soon became my shadow. She watched me to see what she should do. In her face, I saw my own reflected.

Once, at night, I tiptoed into Novenka's room, where she and her parents were both sleeping. I shook her lightly and put my finger to my lips. She awoke with questions all over her face but I had no words to tell her what we were about to do. I just grabbed her hand and led her outside. The cats crawled out of the darkness as soon as they saw me. It didn't matter that a stranger was with me. They came for the food and they came for me. Homeless cats roamed everywhere in our neighborhood. Some had even followed me from the old house, sniffing my trail.

Novenka's eyes grew round.

"Cat!" I pointed to them.

"C-at?" she asked. I nodded.

"Cat!" she pronounced with a grin.

I slipped cheese into her hand and she fed them. They licked her fingers clean. Soon she was naming everything. Cheese. Crackers. Yard. Kitten. Mother. When we were done, I put my finger to my lips.

"No tell! Secret!"

She nodded and pressed her finger over her own lips. We crept back into the house, into our beds, our heads lit up with the words and secret we had shared.

At my new school, Holy Rosary, I soon became the teacher's pet. Our fourth-grade teacher, Sister Theresa, was named after my favorite saint, the gentle "Little Flower." She didn't smile much but she nodded at me with pleasure when she checked my work. I got straight As in reading, literature, geography, attendance and neatness.

I fell in love with language before I was a reader. I knew the power and the mystery language held. The harsh-spoken Croatian, so definite, had authority. Unknown Latin words accompanied by incense, bells, chants and songs were deep and transporting. Latin came from ancient times and called me back there. Language was feeling. I was a listener first.

We had to memorize everything for Sister Theresa. That was the only way literature would become a part of us forever, she taught us. So I walked home, mumbling the sentences, each footstep another word on which I trampled. I got them inside that way. The words lit up my mind and became imprinted there. I recited poetry, without halting, whenever Sister Theresa called upon me. One of my favorites was by Leigh Hunt. It was about a man who believed he was nothing until an angel came to tell him more.

ABOU BEN ADHEM (*may his tribe increase!*)
Awoke one night from a deep dream of peace,

And saw—within the moonlight in his room,
Making it rich and like a lily in bloom—
An angel, writing in a book of gold.
Exceeding peace had made Ben Adhem bold,
And to the presence in the room he said,
'What writest thou?'—The vision raised its head,
And, with a look made of all sweet accord,
Answered, 'The names of those who love the Lord.'
'And is mine one?' said Abou. 'Nay, not so,'
Replied the angel. Abou spoke more low,
But cheerly still, and said, 'I pray thee, then,
Write me as one that loves his fellow men.'

The angel wrote and vanished. The next night
It came again with a great wakening light,
And showed the names whom love of God had blessed,
And lo! Ben Adhem's name led all the rest.

Our teacher loved to speak about the angels. She stood at the front of the classroom with the morning sun falling over her crisp black robes, her face bright and rosy, and named the archangels as if they were her friends. Michael who appeared to Moses in a burning bush. Gabriel. Raphael. Uriel. These beings send our guardian angels to earth, she said. She instructed us to leave a space on our seats so that our guardian could sit there and watch over us. From that day forward, I never sat squarely on my seat.

Then one day, she held up a beautiful painting of an angel.

"This is the Annunciation that Botticelli painted," she told us. "Angel Gabriel visits Mary to tell her she is with child. He brings lilies as a sign of purity."

I remember the shivering all through me when I saw that picture. The long-stemmed flowers she called lilies were the same ones my angel had held. An angel had come to me one night when I most needed him. No one else had seen him. Only Ma believed he was there. Who he was, I never knew. Angels come to tell, Sister Theresa said, to announce. The angel touched us that night but he never came again like I hoped he would.

We wrote stories for composition class. The assignments were boring and nobody talked about what they were going to write. You just had to fill two full pages. Write about a place, our teacher instructed one day. The next day, write about nature. Most kids sat looking up in space, twirling their pencils. I wrote about the trees in Cobalt and my mother's garden there. I wrote about the stars my father saw that I did not remember. The endless snow that first winter I was born.

Sometimes I read my stories aloud in class. We had to. Nobody liked to do it. It was like giving away a part of yourself, almost as if you stood in front of everyone bare-naked. We were all afraid of being laughed at. But the nuns insisted. I could hear my classmates suck in their breath as their name was called. Most kids kept their eyes on their paper, reading in a monotone, so you couldn't catch a word. When it was my turn, I could hear my heart thump all the way up to my ears. The teacher stood at the back of the room and I lifted my voice to reach her.

Sister Theresa's face would soften, her hands clasped behind her robes, pausing in midstep as she listened. She would stare dreamily out the window as if she were visiting Cobalt too.

But I never talked about these things at home. Ma did not want to hear about the past. She always changed the subject if we talked about Cobalt. Maybe, just maybe, if she was in the mood and if Aunt Tracey got her going, she'd talk about her childhood in Calumet. But my brothers and cousins and I told and retold the stories to one another. We wanted to keep the past alive. "Tell me again why our families left Michigan," I'd ask. "Who were the first ones to leave for Canada?" wondered Helen. We eavesdropped on conversations the adults had and carried tidbits back to one another. In the alleyway, our voices buzzed. We put the pieces together like a puzzle we could have never solved on our own.

Chapter 33
The Three of Us

1932

I thought my oldest brother could do anything. He rode his bicycle with his hands in his pockets and a bag of groceries balanced on his thigh, uphill and downhill, over the bumps in the sidewalk. In winter, he wore just a sweater and ran off, hatless, deaf to Ma's cries drifting in the wind behind him. He was always hungry. Sometimes, he found himself far from home with a growling belly and no money. He'd take a roll from the beach bakery, shove it up the sleeve of his sweater and walk out whistling. He was bigger and stronger than William, filled out with muscles, while William was bony and long-legged. The fat could never catch up with William, Ma always used to say, for he moved too fast for it.

My brothers both wore woolen knickers, wide and billowy to the knees, with kneesocks. All the boys wore them. It was like a uniform. It gave them freedom to run and play. They never ripped their pants, just scraped their knees. When Phillip turned thirteen he switched to long pants. By that time, he was a giant. His knickers looked like diapers he had outgrown. William, of course, kicked up a storm at the time because he wanted long pants too. He had to wait, Ma told him. I'd hear him begging her time and time again for long pants, but Ma kept her foot down on that one. Knickers were half the price of long pants. William was in such a hurry to grow up.

Even though I was almost nine by that time, I felt like a toddler beside them, forever trailing in their shadows. I could never catch up with them. Besides, I was too busy to run off. There were always babies to be rocked, milk to be heated and potatoes to be peeled. Endless diapers too. Aunt Tracey gave birth to Jimmy that year and Vinka had Anna. Girls were expected to stay home and help out. I stared from the porch, laundry basket in hand, at my brothers disappearing down the alleyway on their bikes.

We were so different, the three of us. You could tell it just from our haircuts. Of course, mine was the ugliest. Ma cut it herself with a big wooden bowl placed on my head. She trimmed any hair that stuck out beneath it. When she first cut it, I hid for a few days. I didn't look like a girl, I thought, but the boy on the bottle of Buster Brown shoe leather polish. Phillip endured Ma's haircuts too. He sat quietly with a towel around his neck but he refused the wooden bowl treatment. He had such thick hair, Ma couldn't mess it up too much. It fell into curls and waves as it grew in. But my younger brother refused to let Ma touch a hair on his head. She'd threaten to cut it while he was sleeping if it touched his collar. So he'd slam down four cents at the barber every month, money he'd earned from selling newspapers. Ma complained about the waste of money. He wore his thick hair slicked straight back in a pompadour, set in place with grease.

William was the wild one. He did whatever he wanted, stayed out late, shot crap games in the alleyway, stole hubcaps for the fun of it, kissed girls and didn't care what anyone said. Up and down the alleyway, his name was carved into the fence posts. William and Sally. William and Audrey. Ma was steaming mad at him most of the time. William could grin his way through anything, lie through his teeth and look so sweet, you'd want to kiss him. Ma always forgave him, although she knew he'd go out and do the same thing again. Growing up without a pa did that to him. No one and nothing could tell him what to do.

Phillip was quiet. He used to spook Ma sometimes, for he'd tiptoe into the room where she was reading or working alone and he'd sit down so still, she wouldn't hear him. Something would make her look up and she'd jump when she'd see him, sitting there as if he were a ghost. Phillip got a kick out of that. He prowled around like a cat on stockinged feet.

While we were all growing, Ma was changing. I used to look at the wedding portrait she kept on her dresser. It no longer looked like her. She was so tiny, dressed in white from head to toe, her long crepe veil touching the floor and hiding most of her within it. She was seventeen then. She looked the opposite now. There was no softness left in her. No mystery. Just bones. Sharp angles. Her dress hung on her like a potato sack, always loose. Her cheekbones stuck out like rocks.

But Pa had remained forever young. I studied his face, searching it for traces of my own. More than once, I held it up to the dressing table mirror beside my own face and compared our noses, chins, even the wave in our hair. But it was my brother Phillip's face that always stared back at me. His was the face I knew so well. I had Ma's high cheekbones, deep-set eyes and small bones. Even the way my hair fell was like hers, although hers was shot with streaks of gray at the sides now. Phillip was Pa, through and through, Ma said, right down to his voice. It always comforted me to hear that, like a part of Pa remained in plain sight, looking out at us.

There was a place the three of us always ended up, even though we mostly went our separate ways. Far away from the factories, past Landsdown Park, all the way to Grays Road Beach. I rode on the seat of Phillip's bicycle, my hands on his waist, while he pedaled standing straight up as fast as he could. Along the way, he'd call back to me, his words lost on the wind. William rode behind us with a picnic basket on his lap. In the summer, with sweat pouring down our backs, we didn't waste a second once we got there. We'd strip down to our bathing suits and dive right in.

Phillip taught me how to swim. I remember that long-ago day when I first went to the lake and timidly set my toes in. But now, I'd swim out as far from the shoreline as I could go. I stopped only when I couldn't catch my breath.

Then I'd float on my back, drifting away from all the screaming kids on the sand. I could forget anything that way. I swam away from my past. No one could find me out there.

Back on shore, breathless after a cold swim, my body glowed. I'd stretch out under the tall willows and dreamily watch their branches wave high above my head. I'd travel somewhere far away. It was a mystery to me how I could have ever felt sorrowful or worried. I'd look out at the lake and think how God is everywhere. I didn't feel His presence in church as much as I felt it there, in nature.

By the time we left the lake, I'd be cool and clean. Radiant. I'd sing in Phillip's ears all the way home.

Chapter 34
Different from the Rest

1932

Ma and I were digging a patch of dirt in the front yard one summer evening. The soil was sand and slag from the mills. Water ran through it as if it were a strainer. No flowers ever bloomed in that spot. Some of our neighbors had flowers, but they were blackened by soot. Ma tried to plant peonies, but they stayed green and did not blossom. She blamed it on the soot and pointed to Mrs. Chernezski sweeping down the street. The old woman had stopped talking to everyone by then. She cursed at the soot in Polish and held conversations with it like it was a person. She swept all day long. Her son would take her by the arm at bedtime and lead her home.

"No wonder she got like that," Ma sympathized.

A stranger walked by us. He held a notepad in his hand with our name and address written on it.

"Missus Ch..oo..ppp?" he read. "I am Johann Michich."

He was a tall, thin man with a billowy white shirt that blew around his body like a cloud. It was tucked tightly into dress pants that had a crease so crisp they looked as if they could stand up by themselves. He lowered his eyes to study his perfectly polished shoes, as if an answer were written there.

Ma nodded.

He lifted just his eyes up to her then, his light green eyes peeking out from his bowed head. "Missus Chopp, I just arrived from Austria. I need a room. All the good people on this street say to come to you."

He held himself like he was in pain, clutching his hand to his stomach.

Ma pushed her hands through her gray hair and shook her head. "We have no room left in our house. So sorry."

Ma was telling him the truth. Paul slept on the sofa, but I don't think he got much sleep, for babies crawled everywhere. Each room was filled with seven or eight boarders piled on top of one another like ants. Men who worked opposite shifts shared a bed. When one got out of bed to go to work, another climbed in to go to sleep. Although they saved money that way, Ma and my aunt had extra mouths to feed. We ate in shifts, as we had in Schumacher.

"Missus," Mr. Michich said in a thin voice. "Is there not one small corner where I could fit in? I don't need much space. I need a . . . home."

His eyes held hers like they were stuck. Ma could not look away.

"The basement maybe?" he persisted. "They say—your . . . neighbors say—you are kind and that if there's a spot, you will find it."

I thought of the musty root cellar that you had to bend down to get into before you crossed a dirt floor to drag out the potatoes. It was not a spot for a man with a white shirt.

Ma straightened up from her digging. She seemed to be held speechless by the gaze of Mr. Michich. She looked up at the old house, high up to the very top of it. Mr. Michich's eyes followed hers. There was a small space at the top with no room to stand except in the very middle where the roof met. The attic! We had dumped our suitcases there when we moved in and slammed down the trapdoor to it. It was heat heavy up there the spring we arrived. It would be like a swamp now that it was summer.

"Well, I do have something. It's not much," I heard Ma say. "You'll be icy cold in winter. Boiling hot right now. But, if you want it, it's yours."

She pointed to the small window at the top of the house with its view of the gray lake. Mr. Michich's whole thin body stretched up to look. The corners of his mouth lifted like a little boy's into a smile.

"Will I have it all to myself?" he asked Ma.

"No one else would want it," she answered.

"I will take it," he announced. "When can I move in, missus?"

Ma shrugged. It was a mess up there, full of mice too, but she didn't tell that to the new boarder. "Tomorrow," she promised.

That night, Vinka and Aunt Tracey went up to that attic room and cleaned and swept, then set up a dresser, a small cot and a washstand.

The next day, we helped Mr. Michich carry his belongings upstairs. The first thing he did was unpack a case of leather-bound books and place them gently on his dresser. He didn't seem to care about much else. He lined his shoes up under the cot and folded his clothes neatly inside the dresser drawers. His two suits hung from the rafters, where they swung back and forth like lifeless men. By the time we left him, it looked as if Mr. Michich had always lived in the attic. He sat hunched under the eaves, reading books written in German.

Each morning, Ma would leave a pot of boiling hot water on the steps and empty his chamber pot. He never took a real hot soaking bath, just a sink bath at the washstand, a "lick and a promise wash," as Ma called it. But next to the other boarders, he was gleaming clean. He washed and bleached his shirts himself. They were whiter than chalk and stiffly starched, his collar buttoned tight to his neck. He was the only one on the entire block who wore a tie every single day. His hair was greased down and slicked back. His skin was as pale as Ivory soap, for he never stepped into the sun but kept to the shade and to the attic.

My brothers and I had had our fill of boarders by the time Mr. Michich arrived. The boarders seemed to be on one side of the fence while we were on the other. We had learned that in Schumacher.

"Boarders are foreigners. They don't understand English," Phillip always said. "We were born here. We're Canadians through and through."

"Yeah. We were here first," William pointed out.

None of us kids liked the boarders sharing our house, bathroom or kitchen table. We could pick them out as they walked past in the afternoon on their way home from the factories. Big hands. Greasy clothes. Unshaved faces. Dirty from head to toe. But the truth was everyone looked that way. We lived in a neighborhood of workers who had been farmers in the old country. Everyone came from Europe. Cousin Joe, Uncle Jack, Uncle Matt, our grandparents and Pa were once foreigners too.

But we all knew Mr. Michich was different from the other boarders. From the start, I was fascinated by him. He worked as an accountant, tending the books in the office of the steel factory. He was an educated, soft-spoken bachelor, about forty years old. He spoke English in a formal manner. He ate quietly at the table with a napkin tucked into his collar. He refused a second serving. He never wasted his time arguing and smoking in the evenings after work but retired to his room to read. On Saturdays, he'd come down with a handful of letters written in slanted blue script ready to be mailed. He wrote to his family and friends back home every week.

One afternoon, he saw Ma reading bills at the table.

"Missus, do you take care of the bills yourself?"

Ma nodded wearily.

"Here. Let me have a look."

He sat down beside her and arranged her papers. In a ledger, he made neat columns of the figures. He added them up in his head. Soon enough, he figured out what Ma made for the month and what bills she still owed.

"If you're willing to balance my books from now on, Mr. Michich, it would save me a big headache. I'll do something for you."

"Missus, I have a good home here." He smiled. "Let me do your books."

"What about your shirts? I'll bring them to the laundry."

"No. I always take care of my own things."

"When you need something mended or hemmed, I'll do it for you."

"Missus, I learned to sew for myself when I was a little boy."

Ma peered at Mr. Michich's thinness.

"What did your mother bake for you back home?"

He looked up from the ledger then. His eyes filled with tears.

"My poor mama. She used to bake strudel for my papa when he was alive. It was his favorite."

Ma took in a breath, like her whole body was on tiptoe.

"Can I make it for you?" she whispered.

He looked at Ma like he was looking right through her to another place, a faraway country, Austria.

"I will write my mother for the recipe today," he decided.

Within the month, Ma was baking apple strudel like they did in Austria, with thin crispy dough and lots of butter. We ate it every Sunday after church. It always got a smile out of our boarder.

"Thank you, Mr. M!" William tipped his cap at the

boarder as he flew out the door with a chunk of strudel in his hand.

But I stayed behind at the kitchen table. Mr. Michich was reading aloud from *At the Back of the North Wind*. It was an old book from England that we found in the house when we moved in. He was using it to practice his English. As we listened, Ma tiptoed quietly about her chores. The wind lifted the curtains. We waited for each word to be spoken, hanging on a breath. I sat opposite our boarder with my chin on my hands and listened to his thick Austrian accent. I studied his face as he read. It grew softer and rounder. It set a spell on me. I had never heard a story read aloud before. The nuns read geography texts and poetry to us, but they frowned at make-believe books. We weren't allowed to read them in school. They would make us daydream, the nuns warned. Little did they know that the poems had already done that to me.

Chapter 35
Company
Fall 1932

Aunt Elsie came to visit us from Calumet. She was between husbands at the time, Uncle Matt joked. She had just gotten divorced from her third husband and was looking for another. Her kids had to cook for themselves, Ma said. We were dying to meet her.

You could pick her out anywhere. She was the opposite of my mother. Her lips were plastered thick with red lipstick and she had long red nails to match. Even her hair was dyed bright red like Raggedy Ann's mop. She was always puffing away on cigarettes just like the men, a butt hanging from her lips while she filed her nails. She wore high-heeled shoes and stockings every single day. Mr. Michich just stared at her, his jaw falling open, and kept a good distance away.

"You're a Yankee woman," Aunt Tracey teased her.

Canadian women in our neighborhood, like my aunts, wore loose housedresses with bare legs, white ankle socks and sturdy lace-up shoes. They only dressed up for Sunday mass. They hardly ever wore lipstick.

All us kids called Aunt Elsie "Moneybags." She carried her big black leather purse everywhere. To the breakfast table. Into the bathroom. It dangled from her arm at all times. The only time we saw Ma's purse was when she went to church. Ma and her money weren't easily parted.

One Indian summer day, the ice-cream truck tinkled its bell down the street. We scurried from one adult to another and pooled our money for ice cream. One cent from Uncle Matt. Two cents from Ma. Two cents from Tracey. One cent from Joe and Vinka.

"Here, let me have a look," said Aunt Elsie when we stopped her.

We all held our breath. Maybe we'd each be able to get our own cone. I peeked in while she opened her bag. Her hand wiggled inside. She finally pulled out the money. A single penny.

We ran outside quick as we could. Elizabeth trailed at our heels, dragging my Raggedy Ann doll with her. We lined up to split two Dixie cups ten ways.

"What did she have in there?" Helen demanded as we licked our tiny scoop of ice cream from a shared wooden stick.

"Six tubes of lipstick. A mirror," I said. "Powder. Tons of tissues with kiss marks all over them."

"Disgusting!" Phillip spit on the sidewalk.

When Sunday afternoon came, we all piled into Uncle Jack's truck, the kids stacked on top of one another, shoving and yelling in one another's ears the whole fifteen miles to Simcoe. Aunt Elsie had a seat to herself so she wouldn't crumple her good voile dress, but all the other women were piled high with kids' legs and arms. When we got there, Ma sat with her sisters around Aunt Annie's kitchen table. It was the first time they'd all been together since their mother died in Calumet. The men joked you could hear them gabbing all the way across the back field. Even the cows looked up to see who was making such a fuss, they said.

All the cousins played outside. I ran past an open window and heard Aunt Annie say, "It's been almost ten years, Frances. No one wears widow black that long. Only women from the old country."

I stood still by the window, listening. Ma wore her blackness like a second skin. Those mourning clothes were a part of her, like her callused hands and thinness.

"It doesn't bother me any. It's a part of who I am. Just slip on my black clothes every day like they were a uniform."

"It makes you look like an old woman," Aunt Elsie said. "And you're not!"

"Not even our mother would have wanted you to do it," said Aunt Tracey. "Or your husband, for that matter."

Then my oldest aunt told her, "It's time for a change, Frances. Elsie bought you this. We all chipped in."

I peeked into the window. Ma held up something from a fancy box. It was a china blue rayon dress, the color of her eyes. Blooming all over it were tiny red rose-buds. Ma flushed. She stared blankly at her sisters.

"It's a pretty dress, all right. But I can't wear it just yet."

"It's what women are wearing in Michigan," said Aunt Elsie. "I bought it on Main Street in that store our mother used to window-shop at and never step inside. She would have wanted you to wear it."

"Try it on," coaxed Aunt Tracey.

"Nah. I'll just hold it against me."

Ma laid the dress against her body and stood up. It seemed just the right size, swirling down her legs to cover her calves.

"Maybe I'll save it for Baby when she grows up."

"It's for you, Frances. It's your color. Wear it."

Ma folded the dress carefully back into its box and shut the lid.

"Thank you. I'll wear it someday and surprise all of you. But I have to decide on my own when I'm ready to do it."

Aunt Elsie stayed for weeks. She was always itching for excitement. She took Ma to a bingo game, but she had to go to the church social all by herself. No one had time to dance, my family said. Just before she left for Calumet, a neighbor told her there was a fortune-teller downtown. Aunt Elsie offered to pay for everyone's palms to be read.

But my mother didn't want to know about the future anymore.

"If you know the future, you'll stop living here and now," she argued. "If I knew Phillip was going to die young, I wouldn't have married him. I'd have been an old maid. Never had my three kids."

"You need a future," Aunt Elsie informed her. "You're coming."

Aunt Tracey agreed. "You need to laugh. Crack that long face of yours."

They dragged Ma and me both out the door to take the trolley car downtown. The fortune-teller sat in front of a crystal ball in a curtained room. She was a Romanian woman, with wide hips that sagged over the sides of her chair like pillows. A purple kerchief was wrapped around her curly black hair. Whenever her head turned, her gold earrings spun, making a whirring sound like a lawn mower.

"I will first read your past," she announced in a thick accent. "The past predicts the future. Then you can ask one question about your future."

Aunt Tracey was first. She laid her palm in the fortune-teller's wide hands.

"Missus, luck is with you. You have a good husband. You will be married a long, long time. All your lines move ahead. No problems."

Aunt Tracey's mouth dropped open.

"Will I have any more kids?" she asked.

"Be prepared!" said the fortune-teller. "You will have another child late in life. He will always cling to you."

My aunt's eyes almost popped out of her face. She was already too old to have more children, I thought, with her hair so gray and stringy. Uncle Matt said five kids was enough for a stickball team. But I caught my aunt shaking her head as if agreeing.

Aunt Elsie plopped herself in the chair next to the fortune-teller. The gypsy looked down at her palm.

"Lady, you try your luck at everything. Business. Men. Bingo. You are like quicksilver. You have no fear of anything. You must rest more."

"Will I find a wonderful new husband?" My aunt's face turned pink.

"Your heart line looks like a broken chain. You are restless. You cannot stay married long. Just enjoy yourself. Be with people. You will never be lonely. Don't tie yourself down to any one man."

My aunt tapped her long fingernails on the table and frowned. She pushed my mother into the seat next. Ma sat stiff-backed. The gypsy held her palm a long while before speaking.

"Sorrow. Tragedy. Shock." She shook her head. "Your heart line has been cut in half. Your palm is crisscrossed with a million roads. Work. Worry. Children. One life has been taken from you but you will have another life. A long one. You are strong."

Ma sat absolutely still in the gypsy's spell.

"Will she marry again?" Aunt Elsie asked.

The fortune-teller looked straight into Ma's eyes.

"Yes. A star crosses your heart line in midlife. A true friend will arrive from far off. Wait for him."

Ma gasped and looked over at my aunts. They nodded and smiled at her. Ma and Aunt Tracey floated home arm in arm. They could hardly wait to tell everyone on the block. But Aunt Elsie kicked up the dirt beside us with her fancy navy heels.

"What does that gypsy mean, I'm not the marrying type? I've been married three times already."

"Yeah," joked Aunt Tracey. "And divorced three times too."

"I can't help it if it doesn't stick."

"C'mon, Elsie. She said you'll always have fun," Ma teased. "Better than some old husband bossing you around."

Aunt Elsie tossed her head of red curls and laughed. "Maybe that gypsy is right. I like to be the boss."

She linked her arm with my mother's. The four of us skipped all the way down the street to our house.

"Just like we were kids back in Calumet again," laughed Ma.

That night when I asked her about marrying again, Ma shooed me away and said it was all nonsense. It left me wondering. I had seen her pause as the gypsy traced her palm. She lit up too when she'd held the blue dress against her. I could never know Ma through and through. She had secrets, just like me.

Chapter 36
Sickness
February 1933

It was the last week of February, but winter dragged on. It snowed nearly every day and a raw wind blew off the lake through the cracks in the walls. The skies were never blue but always fogged with mist. It seemed spring would never come. Ma looked just like the weather. She came home from the Ideal Laundry just before we went to school. She sank into a chair, her chest sagging. She didn't even get up to walk us to the door and tell us how to behave at school. She had a cold all that winter. She coughed for months. It was plain to see that Ma had lost weight.

"I'm just an old bone," she joked, "that even a dog wouldn't care to chew."

She laughed and that set her to coughing. I couldn't help thinking how old she seemed. Thin and flat-chested. She was only thirty-four years old, I heard someone say, but to me, she looked older. At nine years old, I stretched up tall like a wild weed, while my mother was shrinking.

One morning, Ma was late coming home from work. We were already finished with breakfast when we heard a thump outside. Uncle Matt jumped up and ran out.

There, on the front steps, was my mother, stretched out flat. Her face was grayer than the winter sky.

"Boys! Come out here quick!" he called. "Your ma's collapsed!"

They picked her up and carried her upstairs. She didn't make a sound, not even a moan. Her eyes did not shudder but stayed shut tight. My aunt undressed her and tucked her under the covers. She put her fingers to Ma's wrist. Her lips flattened as she looked up at my uncle.

"Nothing," she whispered.

Then she touched her fingers to where a big vein popped out of Ma's skinny neck and pressed there. We all held our breath, a big circle of kids around the foot of the bed. I was right beside my uncle and I leaned into his body to watch.

Aunt Tracey nodded. "There's a pulse. Very faint. She's scarcely breathing, poor thing."

Uncle Matt cleared his throat. "I'll get the doctor."

The circle gave way then. He and my brothers thudded out of the room, leaving just the girls in a thin, fragile arc holding my mother in. My aunt did not have to ask one of us to leave the room. We were as speechless as the furniture. Even Anna, suspended in Helen's arms, knew not to cry. My aunt pressed cold compresses to my mother's forehead, but Ma did not awaken. Her breaths were so shallow, with long gaps between them, like they were never going to come back.

We waited, the clock downstairs ticking loudly. I could not stop chanting over and over to myself, *Please come soon! Please come now!* I wished I could grab hold of the pointers of the clock and yank them down to make that doctor come.

Finally we heard footsteps in the hallway. My uncle came into the room with Dr. Agro at his heels, his eyes set on my mother. My brothers followed like shadows.

"Frances!" the doctor called to her.

We moved back from the bed, opened the circle, gave way to him. He motioned everyone to leave the room while he examined Ma. My cousins disappeared, then my brothers. My uncle tried to pull me away by my arm.

"*No!*" I jerked my arm away. "She's my ma!"

It was the first time I'd said no to anyone. I planted both feet down on the floor like tree roots. Everyone stared at me. They knew I was not going to budge.

The doctor leaned over my mother, placing a stethoscope on her chest for long minutes. Then he turned her over and listened to her lungs as she breathed. He patted her back with hard cupping motions of his palms. It set Ma into a coughing fit. Her eyes fluttered open.

"Frances, it's the doctor. Sit up high. You'll breathe better."

He propped her up with three pillows. Ma sucked in a short breath and looked at him as if she did not know what he was saying. My aunt handed her a glass of water, but the doctor wouldn't let her drink it until he took her temperature.

We all waited. I held my breath. My aunt tapped one foot. *What's wrong? What's wrong?* The words beat in my head. Surely the doctor must know by now. *Why isn't he telling us?* I felt like screaming, but if I did, they would push me out, away from Ma. I knew I must stand there like a tree and wait for the doctor to be done.

Dr. Agro finally looked at the thermometer and shook his head. All eyes went to him, even Ma's, though she could not speak. She looked as pale as bleached muslin in her winter bed.

"Frances, why didn't you come to me sooner?" He announced in a loud voice, "You've got a fever. A hundred and one."

Ma shrugged.

"Tracey said you had a cold all winter. About how long would you say you've been coughing?"

Again she shrugged.

"Christmas?" he asked. "Longer?"

At last Ma nodded.

"Too long. You've got pneumonia."

Pneumonia! The word fouled the air like a curse. My schoolmate's brother had died of it at Christmas. He was just three years old. The doctor could not save him.

"One of her lungs is full up," Dr. Agro said. "Near collapsed. I'm worried about the other one now."

Ma closed her eyes like she was fading away.

"This woman's going to need care around the clock. You have to watch her every second."

As the doctor gave us instructions, I tried to print them in my mind. But there were so many things—liquids to be taken, medicines, when to cup her back, hot compresses and liniments to the chest, temperature every three hours, turning every hour, broth, a steam machine running day and night—that I couldn't keep it all in my head. His words began to blur. My aunt and uncle listened closely, walking down the stairs with the doctor, whispering. I knew what they said among themselves would be even worse than what they said in front of me.

I was left alone with Ma. She looked up at me. Her eyes were dark and flat. Tears fell, dripping down her face. She swallowed hard to stop them from coming. I reached over and stroked her wet cheeks. Within a moment, I heard the heavy sound of her breath, her mouth fallen open, sound asleep. And all the words I could have said to her just evaporated into the cold winter air.

They would not let me sleep in the room with Ma all that long week. My brothers slept in the living room and I squeezed in between Elizabeth and Jimmy. The bedroom filled with strangeness. Wintergreen. Steam clouds thick in the air. Curtains drawn. Darkness. Footsteps pounding up and down the stairs. Buckets of hot water. Chamber pots. Sheets soaked with sweat yanked off in the middle of the night. My aunt and Vinka, their hair tossed in all directions, wearing yesterday's housedresses, stumbled around sleepless.

My mother lay, tossing in bed, adrift. Then suddenly, at the end of the week, she sank quietly beneath her covers, shutting us out. Her temperature rose. We were all afraid although we did not say it aloud. I saw it in my aunt's long face. I heard it in my uncle's footsteps, no longer heavy in their boots, but tiptoeing.

She drifted four long days. We tried to drip hot chicken soup down her throat, but she'd just drop back down onto the bed, drowning in waves of sleep. She disappeared under our eyes. The doctor said she weighed less than eighty pounds. My brothers weighed more. Her legs and arms were like sticks poking out of the sheets. Her eyes sank in her face like two dark holes.

At night, Phillip paced the hallway outside her room, his footsteps awakening the creaky floorboards in our still house. His hands were two tight fists. "Ma can't go to Pa now, not now," he swore to my aunt. He did not come in with me.

But at least he stood guard. Outside.

Inside my mother's room, the shadows moved close. I could feel something hovering above me, deciding what to do. It watched me too, waiting.

Help must come, I thought, but I did not know how to find it. I seemed to have no voice to cry out. I could scarcely catch my breath. Most of me just faded into the peeling wallpaper. How could the angels come through all this darkness? I worried. Why must I wait so long for someone to save her? But what if the angels did come, and they took her away from us?

"Get better, Ma. Get better." I whispered the words close to her ear.

I tried to pray but no words came. I sat with my head bowed in my hands. I couldn't even look at Ma anymore. She and I were quite alone.

Chapter 37
Between Ma and Me
February 1933

It was a Sunday morning, so early it was still dark. Everywhere about the house, we were stretched out sleeping. On the chesterfield sofa. In stuffed armchairs. In the kitchen, Mr. Michich was clinking china as he put away dishes from the day before. Suddenly the house filled with the thud of Uncle Matt's footsteps rushing down the stairs and out the front door. I flew straight up to my mother's room. One of the boarders stood outside, barring the way.

"Best you don't go in now, child," he said. "Your aunt ordered everyone to stay clear."

He stood between me and the door, his big body filling up the space. I couldn't get past him. I headed back downstairs, where my brothers were stirring. They looked up at me but didn't say a word. I gathered Anna in my arms and squeezed her to my chest. A half hour later, my uncle rushed upstairs with Dr. Agro.

We sat around, everyone wide awake now. Mr. Michich beat eggs in a bowl to make breakfast for the boarders home from the night shift. William paced up and down the rugs. He never was good at waiting. I knew he wanted to run somewhere, hop on his bike, grab a fishing pole and go to the lake. He couldn't go anywhere now. It was harder for him than the rest of us.

Finally Dr. Agro came down. Joe and Vinka walked over to him. Phillip stood in the kitchen, arms straight down at his sides like a soldier. William paused in mid-step on his way out the back door, his fingers falling down on the handle. He turned to look at the doctor.

"She's taken a turn for the worse. Send for the priest immediately," the doctor announced. "I'm going to pick up more medicine. A steamer's coming in from Toronto. They promised me a stronger drug."

The whole room spun around. The smell of eggs cooking made my stomach heave right up to my throat. I dropped Anna into my aunt's hands, for the baby was screaming by then. I clamped my hand over my mouth and ran to the bathroom. I don't know how long afterward it was, but I'd already finished throwing up. I was sitting on the cool tiles of the bathroom floor when I looked up to find Uncle Matt standing there.

"You've had quite a shock."

He looked down at me, his chin sagging, his beard stubble many days old. He bathed my face in cool water. All I wanted to do was cry, cry with my whole body.

"Shhh! Don't cry!" My uncle set his fingers on his lips as he did to shush the young ones. "It'll upset everyone in the house."

He helped me to my feet, wrapped a thick arm around my waist and led me back to the kitchen. Helen, Paul and his steady girl Jenny sat glued to their chairs, unable to speak. A neighbor carried in a pot of steaming chicken soup for Ma. I had a swirling feeling, like I was sinking down. I scanned the room for my brothers. They were not there. Without them, I felt like I was drowning with no one to hear me call. Then I saw the top of Phillip's head outside on the back porch.

I bolted out, freeing myself from Uncle Matt. My brothers sat coatless, side by side, on the bottom porch step, staring gloomily out across the bare yard. There was just the slightest space between them and I squeezed in. We sat and breathed together. Deep long breaths. Then I dared look at my big brother's face. His thin lips had almost disappeared, he was pressing them so tight together. His face was full of muscles, quivering and churning all by themselves. Ever so softly I lay my head on his shoulder in the spot reserved for his girlfriends. Tears fell out of me in a long stream, like a tap left running and forgotten. I cried all the tears my brothers could not.

No one dared disturb us. Everyone stayed inside. My brothers just sat without a sound, on either side of me, listening to me cry.

It was over finally, like a storm had passed. But the grayness stayed behind and would not lift. I went back upstairs and stood outside Ma's bedroom. Only my aunts were allowed inside. Through the door, I heard a rasping of breath scraping over my mother's raw throat. All I could do was pace like a cat on quiet paws in the hallway. Novenka trailed me, full of feelings she had no words for, her eyes reddened.

Then Father Englert appeared, his long black robes swishing around his feet, a crucifix at his belt. He had been called for the last anointing. I knew it was important to receive it in time, to purify the soul before it dies. That's what the nuns taught. But it made me remember how Pa had received it, stretched out flat on a pine plank, already dead. It seemed like the end of the world. My knees wavered. I felt Novenka prop me up on one side and the priest on the other. My cousin squeezed my hand hard, leading the priest and me into the bedroom.

My mother lay thin as paper, propped up in bed, barely breathing. She was almost lost in the steam blowing around her. It was as if she lived in a cloud and all our care and all Dr. Agro's medicines could not pull her back. Our whole family—aunts, uncles and cousins—gathered around her bed on our knees. Father Englert chanted in Latin. My aunt lit two candles, one on either side of Ma's head. They flickered in the airless room. The priest placed a crucifix on one side of Ma and a Bible on the other. He touched her forehead and chest with holy oil in the sign of the cross. He sprinkled holy water over all our bowed heads like tiny tears falling down.

Then the priest closed his eyes for the last blessing. He circled my mother's body with incense, filling the room with puffs of smoke. It burned sweet and musty in our noses.

"God is with you, Frances. If it is His will, return to us healed. If not, go to Him blessed now and free of all sin."

One by one, everyone left the room silently.

Novenka and I were the only ones left, hand in hand. I looked down at my mother sleeping. She was a thread, stretched and worn, holding me to her like an umbilical cord.

I stepped up to the foot of her bed.

"Don't let go! Bring her back!"

I did not whisper it. I hurled it hard as rocks through the air. Beside me, my cousin jerked, she was so startled at the sound.

For Ma had to hear me through the cloud, the mist she lived in. Once before, she had drifted in a vortex and my cry had pulled her out.

It was the only thing left to do.

Chapter 38
Reconciliation
February 1933

t was deep dark when I opened my eyes. I had fallen
asleep on a rug in the hallway outside Ma's room, listening to Aunt Annie's steady footsteps treading back and
forth inside. My aunt had come during the night. Dr.
Agro had brought new medicine too. But the house was
quiet now. No one stirred. I crept to the door and leaned
my head against it. I did not hear anything, not even my
mother's breath. I tiptoed in.

The room was pitch black except for a candle burning
at the bedside. The dark shapes of my aunts loomed in
the corners where the women had fallen asleep. *Please be
alive! Please!* I stood by the bed and looked down. Ma lay
back on the pillows, her face soft, all her wrinkles flattened out. There was no long pause between her breaths
now, no rasp of air against her windpipe. She breathed
gently in and out. Her forehead was cool and dry.

There was rustling beside me, stretching and a yawn.
Aunt Annie stirred awake from her spot at the foot of
the bed.

"Her fever's gone." She sat up. "She's on the mend,
Baby."

I held on to my aunt then and buried myself in her chest like I wanted to do with Ma. I must have cried too although I thought I had no tears left.

"Your ma will get better, child. Wait and see."

In the morning, they pushed all the kids out the door to school. I took one last peek at my mother. She slept on her side, a hint of pink in her chalky cheeks. I sat in school that long day and all I wanted to do was to run back home to check on her. My fifth-grade teacher, Sister Josephine, had to call my name several times before I heard her. I could not do any math problems. The numbers would not stick in my head. I wished I had said something to my mother before I'd left. I had not even dared kiss her good-bye. I didn't want to awaken her. When the last bell rang, I ran home in a sweat.

Aunt Tracey stopped me in the front room.

"Your ma's all right. She was awake this morning and talking. But the doctor told us to let her sleep and not disturb her."

"Let me just peek in the room. I won't talk."

"All right," she agreed. "But let her rest."

I tiptoed into my mother's room and sat in a chair. She was still sleeping, her mouth wide open, sucking in air. It sounded like January wind blowing in from the lake.

Soon my eyes strayed to Ma's dressing table. Pa's picture looked back at us, watching and waiting like me for Ma to awaken. I leaned my head back and imagined how it would have been to have a father. I wondered if we'd still be living in Cobalt. I'd wear a long dress sewn of the calico cloth I saw in Woolworth's, the kind used for quilting. I saw the evergreens tall above me, and me spinning beneath them.

"Baby?" called Ma. "Don't you hear me?"

I turned to her, startled, with clouds in my eyes.

"Ma? Did I wake you?"

"No. I have to get up sometimes." She sat up in bed, her back against the wall. "I can breathe better now."

Ma looked so thin. Her cheekbones jutted out of her face. But her skin was no longer gray. Her eyes focused on me steadily for the first time in weeks.

"What were you doing when I called you?" she asked. "You seemed far away."

"Thinking about Pa." I lowered my eyes.

My eyes must have been shining with tears, for she motioned with one hand for me to come over. I stretched out on the bed beside her. She stroked my hair.

"Why, that's just what I've been doing. I felt as if someone were calling me to get up. To go on. Like Pa once awoke me in Cobalt."

I thought, *Tell me. Tell me*, but dared not say it aloud. Dared not even wonder if the voice she had heard was mine.

We both turned our heads toward Pa's picture.

"I look at that picture and think, he had all his life before him when it was taken away."

"What was it like when he left?"

She sighed and that set her into a coughing spell. I had to sit up until she could breathe again. Finally, she leaned back and I stretched out again.

"I had such a shock when he died. It was like I was standing on the edge of a cliff. I felt I couldn't go on. One night, I woke up and told myself not to think about your pa anymore. I had three kids to care for and only me to do it. I got up and went on with things."

"You never talked about Pa."

"I had to forget him. It was the only way I could think of to get through it."

"You never even told me how you met him."

Ma tilted her head back and laughed softly.

"The first time he came to our house, he came courting for a wife. Our neighbor had told him about us. 'The Brozovich family's got a barrelful of girls. Eight in all. Take your pick.'"

"Why did he choose you, Ma?"

"I was the one who opened the door. I saw him first. I was the third oldest. Annie and Tracey were already engaged or married. It was my turn."

"Why did you want him?"

"He was the opposite of me. I was pale and scared of everything. Phillip was an adventurer. He took me to the tip of the Keweenaw Peninsula to propose to me. He pointed across Lake Michigan all the way to Canada. That's where he wanted to take me, he said, if I would marry him."

She paused then and stared at his picture.

"What I loved most about him was his heart. It was straight as an arrow and set on me. I had no choice but to marry him and follow him wherever he went."

Then she told me how my father made up his mind to marry her. On the way home the day they met, he picked a bachelor's button, a flower growing by the roadside. The next night, it was still blooming as if he had just picked it. It was a sign, he said, that their marriage would be happy.

"Were you happy, Ma?"

She looked down at me and nodded her weary head.

"For all the time I was with him, I was."

She asked me to bring her a tiny wooden case from inside her top dresser drawer. I opened it for her. Inside were a tortoiseshell comb and brass cuff links. They were in our suitcase when we left Cobalt, she said.

"These were his. He had thick wavy hair just the color of this comb. Like your brother's hair."

I picked up the cuff links. A picture was painted on each one in delicate pink and white. A woman's face. She had coppery hair piled up on her head and wore a white lacy dress with a high collar.

"That's me at seventeen. I had these cuff links made as an engagement gift for your pa. It was the style then. I saved my money a long time to afford them."

I smiled at my mother. At last, I knew some of her secrets. The telling brought her more smiles than tears. I think the story surprised her, falling out as soft and gentle as it did. It didn't hurt her anymore.

Flesh and Blood

Winter 1933

A few weeks after her illness, Ma was up and around. She called me into the bedroom one evening to show me something. She had pulled out a carved wooden box from the back of the closet and set it on her lap. Her fingers stroked the old dark wood.

"I don't know why I kept these things so long. I never told anyone about them. They wouldn't understand. Until now. You've been asking."

Tears had fallen down her cheeks, running onto her blouse as she opened the box. I sat on the floor by her chair and looked on, barely breathing. Clothes were folded neatly inside. Old work clothes, worn thin. Stained with dark spots.

"These were your pa's." She touched them. "He wore them the day he died. We buried him in his wedding suit, and this was the last thing I had of him."

She lifted the clothes out of the box as if caressing them.

Pa's overalls. Faded denim overalls with long legs, unrolled at the bottom, and a full, wide chest. They were stained on one side. Darkened. Then Ma held up his blue-and-white-checked shirt. So thin.

"He wore these every day." She smiled, shaking her head. "He never wanted to buy himself new clothes. But we always wore new outfits. Pa insisted."

My hands inched forward to touch the shirt. It was cotton flannel worn so smooth, it wasn't soft anymore, but sleek like a dog's back. The light shone through it. Pa had big shoulders and long arms. A miner who woke up early and worked eleven hours a day. A man who lived in darkness and yearned for the light.

Then I did something that I think animals must do and maybe widows too. I buried my head in that shirt. I breathed him in with my eyes shut tight, surrounding myself with the smell and shape of my pa. Ma set her hands on my head. Her touch drew me back, back to the Cobalt cabin and the shadows above me and how on those forever cold nights, they fell down upon me.

For those moments, knees bent on the floor, he was finally there too. It was like I had my arms around Pa and he had his arms around me.

I remembered Pa.

Chapter 39
Spring in Hamilton
Spring 1933

Ma did not go back to the Ideal Laundry. My aunt would not let her. Vinka went to work instead while Ma and Aunt Tracey ran the boardinghouse. My mother was home all the time now, like I'd always wanted. But she could only do so much. She worked three hours a day and then had to rest. The doctor insisted. She knew we'd tell him if she didn't do just as he ordered. Twice a week, she rode the trolley downtown for heat lamp treatments. Her bronchial tubes were forever scarred, Dr. Agro said. She had to close the windows and stay inside when the factory stoked the furnace.

Ma and I were sitting on the back porch one spring evening after chores were done. The sun had already set but there was still a hint of light in the sky. Dusk, Ma called it, a magical time just before night. That's when the deer in Cobalt tiptoed out of hiding. She'd been wishing to visit Cobalt one more time. A neighbor had been up north and tended Pa's grave. The cemetery was so overgrown, he said, nobody cared for it anymore.

"Cobalt was a bustling place once. A place of new beginnings for so many immigrants." She sighed. "But not anymore. From what I hear, it's just old shacks and poor folks left there."

But it did not feel forlorn in Hamilton that spring. All around us, you could see it. It was the time of snowmelt when all the snow sizzled down and shrank. Just little piles of it stayed behind, in shady spots. Everywhere, the wet brown ground poked through. You knew winter was gone. Aunt Tracey gave birth to Eddie, pale and wide-eyed, and we all fussed over him, for he'd be her last one. Paul married Jenny. They lived a few blocks away, so we saw them all the time.

It was one of those evenings when I first heard the birds sing to one another their good-night songs. All winter they were gone, but now they had flown back. We both listened to their sharp tunes whistling in the trees. Ma pointed to a cluster of yellow daffodils blooming beneath a tree, right beside a heap of old tires. The way they grew there, like a surprise, made the poem pop out of me.

> *I wandered lonely as a cloud*
> *That floats on high o'er vales and hills,*
> *When all at once I saw a crowd,*
> *A host, of golden daffodils;*
> *Beside the lake, beneath the trees,*
> *Fluttering and dancing in the breeze.*

My mother knew the ending of Wordsworth's poem too. She'd heard me recite it over and over again to Mr. Michich in preparation for a school contest that I had won.

And then my heart with pleasure fills,
And dances with the daffodils.

"I miss my garden," she murmured.

"The potatoes!" I said. "From Cobalt."

"You remember the potatoes?"

"You dug them up before we left. They just popped out of the earth."

In a flash, I saw her digging them, their whiteness shining out of the dirt like gold. She had picked them up and dusted their round backs clean.

"Oh, those were my favorite!" She leaned against the wall. "I can close my eyes and taste them now. So sweet."

"I hope we'll have a garden again."

"Not here. Not now." She sighed. "Not in this sandy soil either."

"When?"

"Someday. I saved seeds from Cobalt. Maybe we'll have a farm like your pa wanted. He grew up on a farm. That's what he saved for when he came to America."

"But he didn't get one."

"He had to mine when he came here, Baby. That's the only way he could make money. But he loved to be outside, watching the stars."

We both sat in silence, remembering the stars. I felt Pa all around us, moving in closer, listening. At the mention of his name, even the birds grew quiet.

I had to ask, though it hurt my chest to say the words.

"Did he want to have me?"

I heard the words scratch in her throat. "He always wanted three kids. He was hoping for a girl. He would have been so happy with you, Baby."

I lifted my head to the sky. A star popped out like a diamond, the first star of the evening.

"Make a wish, Ma." I pointed to it.

"I still wish for a farm. Your pa would be happy then."

For those few moments that spring, Ma was just Ma. She had told me what I most wanted to know. I was the daughter Pa wanted. My mother still had her dreams inside her, although she was too busy to talk about them most of the time.

Chapter 40
Poochie
1935

One day, Ma decided she'd like fish and chips for dinner. The best place to buy them was a shack on Beach Road by the lake, a mile away. Millions of seagulls screeched in the fishy air above it, begging for food. They swooped down on the scraps and fought over them, their white wings whirring like those of angels.

I hopped on William's bike that was a foot too high for my twelve-year-old legs, me on the pedals and Novenka on the seat. We rode only a few blocks when we heard the Brightside butcher yelling, "Get away from that garbage!" He was a stout man with bloodstains all over his apron. He kicked a small terrier right in its side.

The dog, skinny and white with black patches, hid in a corner behind the shop after the butcher stormed off. Her tail was between her legs and she hung her head as if she'd lost her best friend. I could see every bone in her body. From the looks of her, she had not seen a home for months.

Novenka tugged my shirt, yelling, "Let's ride!"

But I had my eyes on that dog and I wouldn't let her go.

I wiggled the bicycle toward her. When she noticed me, she scooted away, backing into the corner of the building. She gathered herself into a tiny ball and peeked up at me, her eyes in the top of her head.

I coaxed her. "Tch! Tch! C'mon over here, little baby."

The dog looked back toward the butcher's shop. Oh, I knew she was thinking it was a trap. She remembered his boots.

"If you come with us," I promised, "I'll get you chips. Follow us."

She stood still for five minutes. She kept her eyes on me all the while. Then, ever so slightly, her little tail began to tick back and forth like the arm on a clock.

"Keep on the right side of me, away from the cars," I told her.

Then I rode, the wheels turning. She ran beside me, fascinated by the spinning of the wheels. They spun so fast, they were a blur. She must have seen trucks and trolley buses, big, noisy things, but I don't think she'd ever seen a bike before. I rode slowly at first and then picked up speed. Her head went round and round, following the movement, as if it had become a wheel too. I swear she was smiling. She gave a tiny bark almost as if saying, "Yes!"

Novenka called back to her, "Last one to the lake is a rotten egg!"

The dog came running after us, her paws dancing on the road, making us laugh. She followed us all the way to the lake. At the fish shop, I got off the bike. She stood a distance away, watching.

"If you wait outside quietly with Novenka, I'll sneak you a bite."

She was one long bone looking back at me.

Everyone loved fish and chips. They were English, the fish coated in batter and dipped in hot oil. They sank down into your belly like donuts. The chips were thin and long, sliced from fresh potatoes with the skin still on. They were served wrapped in newspapers. I soon got my order for ten servings.

"Could I have those extra pieces of fish and chips?" I pointed to the floor, strewn with batter and soggy chips.

The owner protested, "You don't want those! They're filthy!"

"But what do you do with them?" I asked.

"At the end of the day, my boy throws them to the gulls."

"Let me do it. I'll give them to the gulls now. They're hungry."

His son swept them up into a newspaper for me. I thanked him and ran outside. Novenka and I hid behind the building, out of view of the shop window. I had promised the food to the gulls. You could love a gull right off, because it's hungry and beautiful. Its cry is insistent. It demands and it gets. Its home was there by the lake, and the fish-and-chip people had learned to live with the gulls as neighbors. A homeless dog was welcome nowhere.

I opened the newspaper wide, spreading it between my outstretched feet. Gulls circled above our heads.

"C'mon over here. I've got something good to eat!" I

arranged the fish and chips. "Fresh-made today. Come and get it!"

The dog leaned forward, sniffing, the little muscles on her chest popping out. I patted the paper, making a crinkling sound.

"You'll like it. C'mon! Don't be scared."

The dog began to tiptoe over.

"Look at her tail," I whispered to Novenka. "It's hopping like a flea."

The dog's tongue crept across the paper. She sniffed her way to a chip. She grabbed it, ran off, swallowed it and came right back. She ate everything and even licked the greasy paper dry. She shook herself off afterward, as if she'd come to life. She looked to be a year old, not fully grown yet. Short-haired and wiry. We threw driftwood to her and she ran after it, bringing it back to us. Finally, she lay down at the edge of the newspapers, her head sunk on her paws.

"Time to go," my cousin reminded me. "Chips are getting cold."

We pedaled home. The dog followed us all the way. We had never owned a pet. It wasn't allowed. I let her into the yard and told her to be still.

"What is *that* thing doing out there?" Ma demanded immediately. "No!" She cut me off before I even asked to keep it.

That afternoon, Novenka and I got a tin tub and soap and bathed the dog in the warm sun. We picked off her fleas, crushing them one by one. Ma looked out at us and shook her head. But later, she brought out dry rags to wipe the dog down.

"It can stay outside, but it can't come in. If she barks, she goes."

I named her on the spot, a name pressing in my head from the first moment I saw her. Poochie. She was small enough to be a circus dog. I'd been to a circus once and a little white dog had performed tricks. It was swift and flexible and I bet Poochie was too. I taught her easy things first: give a paw, stop, heel. Then I taught her to stand straight up on her hind legs. I held on to her paws and she balanced patiently. I'd let go of one paw and she'd stay up, but if I let go of the other one, down she'd topple. Each time I let go, she stayed up five seconds longer. By the end of the week, she stood at attention. All my cousins laughed. Poochie grinned back, sharing the joke.

Then I got a hoop. I made her jump through it, around and around the yard. I'd lift it higher and higher and still she'd keep up with me. When I held the hoop high as my shoulders, she'd rush to the back of the yard to get a head start and then sail right through that hoop. Each time she leaped, I shoved a little treat in her mouth. My aunts and uncles laughed from the porch, as if they had a seat at the circus.

Soon it was November. The nights were cool and damp. I begged my mother to let Poochie inside. "No fleas. No worms. She listens to everything I say."

"I can't have her around the boarders. Or near the kitchen."

Ma let her stay on the back porch. That was a beginning. I began to teach Poochie table manners next. I set up a table with plates. I ate a pretend dinner, talking to her about where she should sit and what she must do.

"No!" I yelled when she set her paw on my lap.

She began to take me seriously when I stopped giving her treats. Then I brought out real food, set it on the table and ate it. Poochie was all eyes, sniffing the air, moving in closer.

"No!" She halted, hearing the tone of my voice. "If you expect to be invited into this house by Ma, you can't come near the table. It is not allowed!"

It took her weeks to learn that trick. She lived for food. Finally, she earned a big steak bone from the garbage. Poochie was ready for the house, but Ma wasn't willing yet.

One day, I dressed Poochie up in baby clothes: a white lacy dress with a bonnet tied under her chin. She looked like a doll. She stood still, patient with everything I did. I carried her outside and slipped her into the bike basket. Novenka climbed aboard and we pedaled down the street.

A car slowed down, driving beside us. The passengers stuck their heads out, laughing. The driver didn't look where he was steering. A truck cut across his path, honking. Poochie barked. The truck driver slammed on the brakes and stared. We howled, winding our way past the truck stuck in the street and the car jammed behind it. Everywhere along the street, people saw us coming and pointed. But Poochie looked disgusted by the whole thing. Her lips were curled up in a black rubber frown.

Car horns hooted. People shouted. Even the trolley bus tinkled its bell at us. Poochie had enough. She leaped out of the basket and ran across the street, her long white gown trailing behind her. The traffic came to a dead halt. Car tires screeched. All eyes followed Poochie.

A woman called out, "What was that?"

A man laughed. "Looks like a monkey!"

"No, it's a baby crawling across the street!" screamed an old lady.

We called after Poochie. For the first time, she wouldn't listen to me. She didn't even look back. She headed home, taking shortcuts through the alleyways. By the time we got to the house, she was on the front porch, barking frantically.

Ma came to the door and frowned. She picked Poochie up. "You didn't take this dog out dressed like that, did you? Poor thing!"

My mother made us undress Poochie and promise never to do that again. She fed her a warm cabbage roll straight from the oven. After that, Poochie lived inside.

I had rescued Poochie from the street, a hungry dog with her tail between her legs. I had found her and she was all mine. She was the first pet I had, the one thing I owned that somebody didn't hand down to me. I chose her.

She studied every movement of my hands as they rolled pie dough or hung up laundry, as if my hands were lamb chops. She followed my every footstep down to the cellar and trailed back up behind me on nimble toes. Her ears tilted back when I spoke to her, as if my words tickled her ears. She licked her lips by my feet, wondering if I'd sneak her a slice of sausage behind Ma's back, somehow keeping one eye on the meat and the other on Ma.

She waited, forever waited, for me to be done. To rush out the door and race through the steel city streets side by side all the way to the lake. Barking and twirling. Jumping up to my chin like a circus dog. Spinning in midair as if she had wings.

An animal will let you love it through and through. No matter if you're sad or angry or too busy to pat its head. It'll wait for you. It'll love you right back too. No questions asked.

That dog was surely in love with me, everyone said.

Chapter 41
The Tan Suit

Easter, 1936

I was never interested in clothes. I suppose it was because we couldn't afford new ones. Besides, I believed that I was plain as a brown nut and no clothes could change that. But I noticed Helen's outfits all the time. She worked in the office at the steel company. She had plenty of boyfriends. They'd pick her up at the house, so my uncle could give them the once-over, and she'd look perfect. She painted her nails and lips coral, piled her hair up high and wore heels. She had a dazzling smile, big white teeth and a wide mouth made for laughing. Uncle Matt said she looked like a million dollars. But he wasn't allowed to say so in front of her boyfriends.

One of the neighbors offered Ma a suit. Size four. Tan gabardine with a fancy label from Toronto. Trimmed all around the lapel and pockets with gold embroidery. No one in our house could fit into it, although everyone tried to. It was too tight for everyone and much too long for Ma.

"Baby, come over here." Ma laid the suit against me. I was almost thirteen at the time, the biggest tomboy on the block. "Why, it's just your color. It sets off your hair. But it's miles too big."

I tried it on and stood on a chair. Ma popped a pile of straight pins into her mouth, mumbling at me to turn slowly around in a circle while she pinned. She tucked in the waist, shortened the sleeves and deepened the darts everywhere. She worked on it for a week. I had to run in from a game of tag or hopscotch, all sweaty, and try on that suit every single day. It was wool and it itched my bare skin. But there was no saying no to Ma.

We went shopping downtown for a hat to match the suit at Eaton's, the best department store. Ma pointed to a wide linen hat with silly flowers on top. It flopped on my head like an old lady's hat. It was three dollars. That was a splurge for Ma. But I searched until I found the hat I wanted. A brown felt beret with a tiny green pheasant feather riding on the side. It fit me perfectly. The sales-lady said I could wear it year round with my suit. In the end, Ma was convinced. The beret cost two dollars.

I could hardly wait for the chance to wear the new outfit. On Easter Sunday, it was cool and windy, a great day for a suit. I borrowed real silk stockings from Helen, holding my breath as I wiggled into them. For the first time in many months, I didn't wear my long winter coat. I felt light and free and a touch naked because I wasn't all bundled up.

When I walked into the kitchen for breakfast, every-one was seated already. I had taken an hour to dress. I had never done that before.

"So pretty!" Novenka called out.

"Who is this beauty?" asked Aunt Tracey. "Why, it's Frances! You've grown up overnight. Turn around and let's have a look."

And so I did to a tune of low whistles from William. Margaret's and Elizabeth's eyes were glued right on me, following my every movement. Even Eddie had something to say. He gurgled at me, his mouth full of oatmeal.

Helen yelled like a cheerleader, "You're perfect!"

Ma was beaming. She had taught herself to mend and alter clothes like a dressmaker. She could turn hand-me-downs into a perfect fit. It hadn't cost her a cent either.

"Where did you get all those curves?" demanded Helen. "Your waist is almost not even there."

I looked down but couldn't see a thing.

"That's a movie star figure," said Aunt Tracey. "Look in the hall mirror and turn to the side, Frances, and you'll see what she means."

I stood in front of the full-length mirror. The suit fit me like a glove; the darts pulled in at the front and sides, giving me a figure for the first time. It looked like I had breasts and hips when I didn't have much of anything to brag about. I stared at myself. The suit had transformed me. Like magic, it made something out of nothing.

"Wish I could find a suit that would do that to me!" My aunt laughed and everybody roared.

"You're lucky to have that shape," Helen said admiringly. "You're just like your ma. Petite."

"What's petite?"

"It means you're not like us." My aunt grinned. "We've got extra. Big hips. Wide waists. Full busts. Tall too. We take after my pa's side of the family."

"Petite is tiny, that's all," said Ma. "Short. Skinny. Been like that my whole life. That's how my mother was too."

Vinka nodded and laughed. You could see all her gums when she did that, for she had no teeth left. Even she had noticed the new me. You wouldn't think she would pay any attention to such things. She was almost six feet tall and wore overalls most of the time. She could outwork both Ma and Aunt Tracey together at any task, from beating rugs to cooking a ten-course meal. She spoke to me in Croatian and all the women laughed.

"She said you look like a doll, Frances, all dressed up."

I gave Vinka a kiss on the cheek and we all left for church. I felt like skipping all the way there. Poochie jumped at my heels, pointing her tail up, like she was sailing through her hoop. Everyone's spirits were high. On the street, we passed a newsboy delivering the morning papers. He wore his cap at a jaunty angle, whistling a tune. He looked me up and down, turning his head back to stare while he walked straight ahead. He almost fell into a tree, then stumbled down the street to stand up. Everyone burst out laughing.

The tan suit changed who I was. I was no longer a brown tomboy. I was petite. I could hardly wait for more spring Sundays and the chance to wear the suit again. I let my Buster Brown hairdo grow out, and I let Helen pin my damp hair up. The next day, instead of straight hair, I had deep, flowing waves just like her. She gave me two sequined barrettes to hold my hair back. Uncle Matt teased me by saying Croatian girls seemed to grow up overnight. One day they're playing jacks, and the next day, begging for silk stockings. That made me blush.

I was becoming someone new. I didn't have to wish for it, or sit on staircases, yearning to be elsewhere. I was Frances. That's what Ma called me now, not Baby anymore.

I remembered how Pa had a secret name all picked out for me but he never told my mother. He hid it like a shiny chunk of silver, waiting for his firstborn girl to arrive. A girl named Frances.

It was the name Pa picked out, I'm sure.

Chapter 42
Frank
1936

That spring, Mr. Michich had a tragic accident. His car slipped off a rainy road along the escarpment and tumbled down a ravine. We never got to say good-bye. Ma said he was the only boarder she had made friends with among the hundreds she had cared for. We wrote to folks in Austria to tell them the news. Since his mother had already died, he had no family left. In the attic, we packed up his belongings, waiting for word about whom to send them to.

The house grew quieter. Joe finally bought a farm on the top of the escarpment. He worked at the steel company while Vinka tended the animals. Their new baby, Pauline, was born there, and Novenka was like a mother to her. We visited them on Saturdays sometimes. In the summer, my family helped them harvest, all the cousins running behind the tractor, bundling up hay or corn or potatoes onto the wagon. But we always had to go home and leave them. Novenka would wave at me, a small figure by the barn, the baby in her arms.

I hated to pass by their old bedroom in our house. Six new boarders were crammed into that room. I remembered how Novenka and I had stretched out on the bed and told each other stories about Cobalt and Severin. We talked on and on. Novenka was more than a cousin. Something had set between us like cement before we'd even met. We had called out for each other.

Aunt Tracey and Uncle Matt began to murmur that they wanted a house of their own too. Everyone except us was moving on. Then Phillip began to disappear. I was the only one who knew where he was. He had met a Croatian girl, Mary, at the beach. She was thin and tall with wavy blond hair. It turned out she had been born up north like us and now she lived only a few blocks away. Phillip swore me to secrecy about his steady girlfriend. He wasn't ready to tell Ma yet.

Early one July morning, someone rapped loudly at the front door. Hardly anybody used that door. Deliveries, boarders and friends came and went by the side door. The front door was formal, with wavy glass set in thick oak, too heavy to open. I ran to answer it, knowing it would be a stranger. A European man stood on the porch, his hat in his hands. I could tell he was straight off the boat. A shiny leather suitcase stood at his feet, and he was dressed up in his Sunday best on a workday. His suit was thick wool and his leather brogues were carefully polished. Only his face didn't shine. It was pale and serious. He wore thick glasses with the widest blue eyes I had ever seen. It was his eyes that I stared at, for they were misty, like the wind had blown too hard. They were full of tears.

"Are you looking for a place to board?" I asked the gentleman.

"No. I will find a place . . . soon. But—I come to speak to Mrs. Sh-Sho-op?" He spoke with a thick accent, struggling to say our last name.

"Chopp," I answered. "Where are you from?"

"Austria." His lips fell into a sad smile.

I invited him into the hallway and ran for Ma, instead of shouting to her as I usually did. I thought all along the way that he reminded me of Mr. Michich. His smooth-shaven skin. His straight brown hair carefully slicked back. Even how he stepped inside, his brogues tapping lightly on the hardwood floor. I had a strange feeling, like the world had stopped spinning and everything slowed down for just this moment when the stranger entered our house.

"Mrs. Chopp," he said when he saw Ma, "I'm Frank Stampfl. You wrote to me some months ago about my poor friend Johann."

"Oh, you've come about Mr. Michich's things?"

Ma had set aside piles of books and clothing left by our boarder. I stared at Mr. Stampfl. Mr. Michich had told us stories about him. The two of them had grown up together in Austria. Mr. Stampfl had often written here. I even recognized his handwriting, thin slanted script, in tiny letters. Mr. Michich had always smiled when he received mail from his friend.

Ma invited Mr. Stampfl into the living room and brought the boarder's belongings out to him. He touched the books and shook his head.

"I should have come to America sooner," he confessed. "For years, Johann begged me to join him. But I stayed home, helping my parents cut wood for the mill. I could not leave that place. Until now. My family has passed on and so has poor Johann."

By that time, he was sipping English tea with five spoonfuls of sugar, studying Ma's face. She told him how kind Mr. Michich was and about his life in Canada. Mr. Stampfl told her about the forest where he lived, the tiny log cabin lost in the tall evergreens. It was built by his family on a lake where they cut logs in their own sawmill and sailed them downstream. Ma studied him back, a teacup on her lap, listening to his stories. Soon she was telling him about Cobalt and our cabin and the vast wilderness, which she'd been so afraid of, on all sides of her. He said he was never afraid in the forest. A man could never be alone with all that beauty. But here, in this busy city, he felt alone. When I tiptoed out of the room, neither of them noticed.

When he finally said good-bye to my mother, they shook hands.

"I see you are a caring woman." He thanked Ma, books under his arm. "You took care of my old friend. He found a home with you."

"And you are a caring man, a true friend to Johann. It is good you came."

Mr. Stampfl walked off with his suitcase. Ma had given him the names of several boardinghouses that might have a room for him. Mr. Michich's room had been taken over by my brothers. Boys needed their own space, Ma said. She stood at the open doorway, watching the Austrian gentleman disappear down the street. He walked slowly, light on his feet, lost in thought.

"He had cold hands." She smiled. "Cold hands, warm heart. That's what my mother always said."

A week later, Mr. Stampfl came calling again.

"Mrs. Chopp, I came to thank you. I am staying the next street over. The whole house is filled with Austrians, just like you said. Mrs. Werner cooks like my mother."

"Come in. I'm pleased you like it."

He was dressed in everyday clothes, khaki colored, but they were sparkling clean and neatly pressed.

"I found a job at Canadian Industries Limited. As a carpenter."

Ma was smiling now. She invited him into the kitchen to sit at the table with everyone.

He came over once a week after that, on a weekend evening, and Ma always served him apple strudel. She was calling him Frank by that time. He never liked to see her work on weekends.

"Frances, you work too hard. Sit down and eat strudel with me," he'd beg her.

Ma usually socialized as she worked. She ironed or folded laundry and still kept up with the conversations. She was always in a race with time. But she wasn't like that with Frank. She dropped everything when he came. The two of them got so wrapped up in talk, I had to finish cleaning up the kitchen by myself. She usually never sat down until dusk, when the two of us grabbed some moments alone.

But now Mr. Stampfl stayed on late. Soon as I saw him at the door, I knew I had lost Ma for the evening. So I hurried through my chores and ran off down the alleyway to play with the neighbors, missing Novenka more than ever. Even Poochie abandoned me. She wouldn't stop barking until Frank patted her head. Then, she settled in right by his shoes, examining his every movement, ignoring me.

That summer, Frank appeared every evening after dinner was cleared away. He sat outside on the front porch. Ma brought him a cup of coffee and sat beside him. He practiced his reading aloud to her, like Mr. Michich had once done, only he read from the newspapers and told her what was going on in the world. He was forever explaining politics to her, like the war between Japan and China and the unrest in Europe, and the way it was here because of the Depression and the war. He liked the American president Roosevelt. Roosevelt believed he'd find a way to make America strong again. That would help Canada, too, since we were its neighbor. Soon, Frank would apply for his Canadian citizenship. He had decided to stay in Canada, like his old friend.

Helen and I were in the kitchen one evening, cleaning up.

"Frank's courting your ma," she notified me.

I peeked out the window, my head beside hers, a tea towel in my hand, and watched the two of them. They looked so serious.

"Is that called courting?" I asked. "Reading the news-paper out loud?"

"To them it is. It's their way of getting to know each other. Besides, did you ever see your mother sit next to a man before?"

I began to study Ma more closely. One Sunday, she came down to breakfast in the outfit her sisters had bought her years before. In that blue dress, she looked years younger, as if she'd turned the clock backward and became the woman she used to be. She even curled her hair in pin curls at night and touched it up in the morning with blue gel. She went to the beauty parlor to have it cut once a month instead of doing it herself. She sent all her black clothes to Croatian widows in the old country.

She had become a different person. Not quite as skinny or dark, she hummed to herself as she moved about her chores. I would even catch her smiling to herself at times.

Frank kept coming around, night after night. By October, it grew colder. They could no longer sit outside. They seemed to have gotten used to each other's company by then. Ma ironed in the kitchen while he talked to my aunt and uncle. I always listened awhile before I disap-peared outside. I felt awkward at first around Frank. He didn't come to see me, I thought. But he'd pat the chair next to him to sit down and ask me how I was doing at school. So I'd sit, twirling my hair in my fingers, hunch-ing my shoulders. He never said much, but he smiled like he admired me. He always complimented Ma for having a beautiful daughter and two handsome sons, but he would never say so to us.

I realized that Frank was just shy, more so than Mr Michich had been. Soon enough, I was reciting poems fo him as I had done for his old pal. He'd lean back quietly in his chair, studying me closely. I told him all abou Cobalt too. Nobody could get a word in once I startec talking to Frank. He was a good listener, Ma said. And had so much inside to tell that I had never said aloud.

Frank began to fix things next. He'd sit down at th table to examine our broken things, things on the way t the garbage. First it was Ma's toaster, then the brakes or Phillip's bicycle, then William's watch and then a broker necklace I'd found. No matter how badly something wa. broken, he always found a way to fix it. He'd sit wrappec up in a kind of spell when he was fixing things, a lit ciga rette stuck in the corner of his mouth, staring intently a the broken thing. He wouldn't put it down until it wa. repaired. His coffee grew cold. We had to remind him tha his cigarette had burned down, six inches of gray ash dan gling from his lips. Ma laughed and called him Fix-it Man

Ma was the one who could make something out o nothing, like the way she spun the sweetest strudel from flour and eggs. But Frank turned our broken nothing: back into somethings. By that fall, it was plain to see, th two of them were a pair.

Looking back, I remember how we'd always been giver a sign that change was coming. I knew it in an instant With an omen. Cousin Joe's footsteps in our shadowy cabin. Aunt Annie's letters about southern Ontario. Th crows darkening the sky the morning Pa died. And now

rank. He'd come into our lives so quietly, with a knock
n the door and tears in his eyes. He had a way of soften-
1g everything around him, especially Ma.

For Christmas, he gave me a wooden pencil case that
e'd made. On the lid he had carved a row of evergreens
rith a tiny cabin underneath, just as I had described
:obalt.

"You like to write," he said. "Keep your pencils safe
1 here."

He whittled the ends of all my pencils, including the
olored ones, to a sharp point. I could hardly wait to use
1em. They just glided over the paper that way.

"Frank's courting you too," Helen observed.

We both giggled at the thought.

Chapter 43
Riding Out
Summer 1937

Once we had been a house of girls. But I was the only gir
left at home then. Aunt Tracey and Uncle Matt finall
bought a house on Gage Avenue, a half hour's walk away
Helen got engaged to her steady boyfriend, Stan. I wave
good-bye to the last of our cousins. Even Raggedy An
moved on, squeezed tight in Eddie's hands, to quiet hi
tears. We didn't fill the empty bedroom with more board
ers either. My brothers took it over, after freezing all win
ter long in the attic. Everyone had a place except me.

Something brewed inside me, a restlessness to mov
on too. I was thirteen by then, but Ma wouldn't let me g
anywhere alone. I had to walk everywhere or beg Willia
for his old bike. But he was always off with it somewhere
I wanted to go out on my own, in spite of Ma's worrie
More than that, I wanted to get to Novenka.

I decided I needed a bike of my own. I bugged Ma a
winter for one, but she said we couldn't afford it. We'
look around for a used one, she said, that a neighbor's ki
grew out of. I was tired of borrowing old rusty bikes wit

tires that had more patches than rubber. I wanted a new bicycle. I kept on.

I didn't wear my mother out with all my pleading though. It was Frank who couldn't take it anymore.

"Take a look outside, Frances," he announced when he arrived one spring Saturday morning. "Something's waiting for you."

In the backyard, a metallic blue bicycle glittered in the bright sun. A brand-new CCM built for a girl. I raced out. It had a wicker basket, cushioned seat and a tinkly bell. My very own bike. I hugged Ma and Frank and rode circles all over the yard. I whooped it up so loud, all the neighbors hung out the windows in their housecoats to see what the racket was about.

"When can I go to Novenka's?" I yelled to Ma. "Bet I could get there in an hour on this bike!"

My mother's lips flattened. I could tell she was steaming up inside about my going so far on my own, but she didn't want to make a fuss in front of Frank. She had to be a lady in front of him. I looked straight at Frank as if to say, You bought me this, now what?

He sneaked a look at Ma, then shyly slipped his arm around her shoulder. "Let her go, Frances. Here's what we'll do. We'll give her a head start and drive up in a while to visit your cousins. See how she makes it up that hill. We can drive her back home if she's tired."

Ma's face softened. "First, she'll eat a good meal. Then I'll fry some spareribs with sauerkraut and bring it to Vinka's for our lunch."

I was gone in a half hour, my mind racing far ahead of my legs, eager to get there. First I rode along Gage Avenue, where I waved to my cousins so that they could admire my bike. Then I took King Street out of Hamilton, my tires whirring so smooth and fast, you couldn't even hear them. When I reached the country where the street met Highway 20, I stopped.

Ahead of me rose the escarpment along the highway. Everyone called it "the mountain." I had always laughed at that name until I stood alone at the steep bottom of it, looking up. It curved up and never stopped. I couldn't see the top. Trucks chugged up it, blowing smoke all the way, coughing and struggling. I pressed down on the pedals with all my weight, but my bike hardly budged. It felt like a hunk of steel. Even when I stood straight up it creaked slowly. So I got off and walked, pushing it, my eyes straight ahead to the top. Frank passed me and slowed down but I waved him on. I finally made it up. I bicycled along Ridge Road at the top of the escarpment, winding past huge farms and cows grazing in the fields.

Novenka was waiting for me at the tip of their half-mile driveway. She wanted a bike as soon as she saw mine. She climbed aboard the seat and I pedaled her home. Everyone was so amazed I had made it up the mountain. It had taken me three hours to get there. I ate everything in sight, gobbling down the spareribs. Joe gave me advice about going back down. He rode his bike down to work at the steel company every morning at five A.M.

"Keep your back and head down flat. Watch out for rocks. They'll throw you right off that bike. Pump your brakes gently long before the bottom. Otherwise, you'll sail right into the lake."

Everyone laughed except Ma. If we'd been alone, she would have made me pile my bike into the car with her. She ordered Frank to wait at the bottom though, in case there was trouble.

I pedaled back to the highway. I stood alone at the top, my heart gathering speed with the traffic. The road led straight down at a dizzy angle. Trucks boomed past me, honking warning sounds. I sucked in my breath and started the pedals rolling. I never touched them again. The road took me down, faster and faster, until I was speeding on that CCM past all the trucks and cars. I flattened my body out and held on tight. I must have started to scream about halfway down when I saw the lake, my mouth opening so wide, I captured a breeze right down my throat. I could feel my hair stream out behind me as if I were riding in an airplane with the top down. At the bottom, I didn't have to stop. The traffic light was green. I sailed past Frank's car parked there, my mother's head sticking out the window, yelling something I couldn't hear. I got home before they did, my whole body glowing. I had outraced all the cars.

From that day, I was hooked on bicycling. As soon as I set my hands on the handlebars, I felt like going somewhere. That bike had power. It could take me places I had longed to go. On that bike, I could be on my own for the very first time. I just climbed on and zoomed away.

When school was finally out, I could ride anytime, not just on the weekends. Soon as I had the chance, when chores were done, I'd be off. To the lake. Downtown

Hamilton. Poochie hopped at my side, yapping all the way. I'd pretend I had somewhere important to go, racing ahead, but mostly I turned around when I got there. The fun was the journey, the pedaling hard up the hills without stop, the rush downhill, getting back in record time, the breeze cooling me down on hot humid days.

I thought back to Schumacher and how the world had dwarfed me in my dark corner. How I couldn't get to it. Now I explored everywhere. I saw the city of Hamilton from the back of my bike, watching it pass by slowly, people going places, and me passing them all.

There was one place I was burning to go. Aunt Annie's farm in Simcoe, fifteen miles out, up the mountain and then along a dirt road, in the opposite direction of Vinka's. Ma finally said yes. It was soon arranged. I'd stay overnight too.

It was a hot summer day when I rode out. I loved going up the mountain. Although I still had to walk my bike, it took me half the time now. At my back, Hamilton lay dusted in soot and factory smoke, disappearing in the distance. Ahead of me stretched the flat beige farmland I'd heard about all my life. Cool old maples shadowed the roadside. When I turned into the long familiar driveway, Lady hopped out to greet me, but not right away. She was old now, almost blind. She had lost a front leg chasing cars down, but she still knew me and could give the ground hogs a run for their life. I must have looked a mess, for when my aunt saw me, she made me change and told me to sit down on the shady porch with a lemonade. I was soaked with sweat all the way through my clothes.

The farm had a quietness, a calmness, that we never had in our house. I felt it immediately. During the day, my aunt and I worked around the house. We churned butter, the spinning of the wooden handle making a steady thump. Killdeers called. Noon spun a hot silence of yellow sun. At dinnertime, Uncle Jack and the boys still living at home washed up outside and sank into their chairs at the table, blessings said, heads bowed. Seven of us around the table. Not one word spoken during the meal. Afterward, Uncle Jack pushed back from the table, lit his pipe and took stock of the day. About how much longer they could keep the thrasher running. A wish for the rain to hold off. Thirty acres still left to hay. Simple things.

We talked around the table until darkness fell bit by bit, until Aunt Annie lit the kerosene lamp, and we tidied up in slow motion, all of us going to bed early. My body sank deep down into the covers, asleep before I shut my eyes.

My aunt was always someone I didn't have to say much to. When I left the next morning, she packed my basket with a cold lunch and gathered me against her.

"I remember the day I first laid eyes on you. Look how you've grown. Taller than the sunflowers. Prettiest girl in the family too. Strong and brave to pedal all the way out here to visit me."

When she released me, I felt a seal had been set upon me. I believed not just that her words were true but they came from noticing, from love. I wasn't invisible anymore. I was my own girl. A brand-new girl on a brand-new bike. I felt so energetic that instead of riding home, I headed straight to Novenka's. There, by the barn, stood her new green bike. She rode back with me to the top of the mountain road. Everything was set. She'd meet m at the bottom next Saturday. We'd ride out together to se the fruit belt along Highway 8 as far as we could go. W had heard how beautiful it was.

Ma approved of that plan because I wouldn't be goin up the mountain. But she set a curfew for returning tha was much too early. That highway stretched for mile and miles along the flat land. It'd be easy to pedal it th whole day long.

"Go on ahead, Frances. Enjoy yourself." Frank winke at me. "I'll take your ma out to the bingo game Saturda night and she won't care what time you come home."

Ma laughed and slapped Frank on the arm. She love to gamble, at cards and all games. She always came bacl from bingo games with money in her pockets. She ha never lost a cent. She was someone willing to take chance, Frank teased her, on cards, and on an old bachelo like him.

It was Frank I had to thank for my newfound free dom. He had not just given me a bike. He had steppe into the spot beside Ma where I had always been. It ma have bothered me at first, it was so unexpected, but then felt a burden fall from me. There had never been anyon except me to worry about her or calm her. I didn't have t do it anymore. Frank would.

Novenka and I rode out along Highway 8, a pave road with a grassy path beside it for riding. It bustle with trucks carting fruit and day pickers to and from th orchards. The fruit belt was a narrow strip of land squeezed between the escarpment and the lake, just past Highway 20, stretching all the way to Niagara Falls. The sun just beat down out there. No shade on the side of the road. We got boiling hot and stopped at a farm stand on the road past Stoney Creek. We bought a quart of free-stone peaches that split open with a twist, then gobbled them down, the peach juice melting down our faces like syrup. The fruit was pure summer, the taste of hot sun and sweetness mingled.

We sprawled out afterward in the shade of an apple tree, surrounded by acres and acres of fruit trees and vineyards. Concord grapes still green. Bartlett pears. McIntosh apples in first blush. Plums. Black cherry trees loaded with dark red fruit. Raspberries. Apricots. We wanted to eat it all.

It was a slice of heaven in that fruit belt. I thought how Pa would have liked it out there, where things grew. He would have hated to live in the soot and grime of industrial Hamilton.

We pedaled on, hoping to reach the falls, but at St. Catharines we had to turn around. The sun had sunk behind some clouds and the western sky was bright red. It was almost dusk. We rode, pumping without stop, straight into the sunset, our hair blowing back to the fruit belt. Just the rhythm of the two of us, going places side by side, was enough.

Next summer, we promised each other we'd join the day pickers like my brothers now that we had our own bikes. Until then, we rode out every chance we got. I fell asleep most nights that summer still pedaling, the wheels spinning on ahead in my dreams.

Beauty was not close by, where I needed it. I had to ride out to find it.

Chapter 44
Proposal
Fall 1937

I remember sitting in the car that autumn day when Frank drove my mother, Helen and me those same ten long miles along Highway 8 to Stoney Creek that I had pedaled with Novenka. On one side of us, the escarpment rose up. On the other side, we caught glimpses of Lake Ontario, tossing with waves as if it were laughing. The road seemed to go straight along the flat land for endless miles. Acres of fruit trees bordered the road, just as we had described them to Ma. It was her first time out there. Frank pointed out the dark-limbed cherry trees beside the rough-skinned apple bark, and the solemn tall brick Victorian farmhouses with etched windows and peaked roofs.

Finally Frank slowed down and pulled the car over to one side.

"There it is." He pointed. "It's what I've been looking at."

It was just woods on both sides of the road. Flatness. Brush and weeds. Nothing. Frank asked us to get out of the car. We followed him a distance from the road. It came to us gently at first, then louder. A gurgling. Below the field in a wild, overgrown gully was a creek, wide and muddy.

"That's the border of the property I'm looking to buy," Frank said. "Someone started a vineyard here once but abandoned it. We could make it grow again."

My mother's eyes turned sharply toward his.

"I've been out here several times. Looking. Planning. It's twenty-five acres of flat land, Frances. I could build a strong brick house. Right over there." He showed us a mound of land, half cleared, where an old oak rose up.

"We'll have neighbors soon." He pointed across the road to a wide stretch of land. "A church is coming. A school. And a library too."

Ma was quiet, her hands weighing down her pockets, her wool coat drawn tight to her body. A raw wind whipped at our faces, so we all piled back into the car. Frank leaned over, wrapping his arm around the back of Ma's seat. Helen and I squeezed together in the backseat. We both kind of waited, holding our breath, knowing we shouldn't say anything.

Frank was a shy man, that's what I knew about him, but he was doing all the talking that day. It took him a while to make up his mind and even longer to speak his mind. Usually, Ma made the decisions for everybody. She even answered her own questions. But she had been strangely quiet on this trip. In her seat, she looked small, like a cornered mouse.

"Frances, do you know what I'm trying to tell you?" Frank finally spoke up.

Ma looked down at the floorboards as if examining her shoes. She slowly raised her eyes, yet didn't say a word.

"Frances . . . I'm trying to say that . . . if you're willing, why, I'd—I want you to marry me."

He took hold of Ma's hands.

"I'd like us to move out here. Sell the boardinghouse. I plan to build that brick house for you and your kids. Frances is young enough to stay. She's welcome and so are your sons. I'll make it big enough for all of us."

I could scarcely trust what my ears were hearing. A house in the country along the fruit belt. Orchards all around us. No more soot. No more boarders.

He leaned back and sighed. "We'll have a farm, Frances, like you always wanted. Peaches. Cherries. Lilacs. Peonies. A garden. Chickens too."

I heard something then, a sharp sound like a gasp at the back of my mother's throat. She turned toward Frank, tears rolling down her cheeks. She swallowed hard. For the first time, I could tell she didn't know what to say. Helen, who had been poking me in the ribs and pressing her knees harder and harder into mine, was mouthing silently to me, "Say yes! Say yes!" I was afraid she would burst and scream it out loud, but she didn't.

I held my breath, watching Ma's face change. The last bit of hardness she'd kept there for fifteen long years slowly melted away. Her lips were soft and full, not drawn flat in her usual frown.

"Yes, Frank. I'll marry you," she whispered. "I've been waiting for you to ask."

We both let go in the backseat like balloons bursting. We thumped the upholstery with our fists and screamed up a storm. My head hit the roof, I was jumping so high. Frank hugged Ma and they turned to look at us as one person instead of two separate ones. Their heads were touching and they were both smiling.

I thought back to the fortune-teller Ma had visited. A true friend would arrive in midlife, she had predicted. Ma was forty years old now. She had thought her life was over long ago. But Frank had traveled all the miles from Austria to Birmingham Street just to find her. And me too. Somehow he had known the way.

Chapter 45
A New Beginning
Summer 1938

In the summer of '38, when I was almost fifteen, I was finally old enough to become a day picker at Corman's orchards. I rode out shivering in the cool mornings, when fog still hugged the land, the dew curling my hair. The trip was only twenty-five minutes long. Side by side with Novenka and William, I picked fruit as it ripened, moving from field to rolling field leading up the escarpment. Bing cherries. Sour cherries. Shilo yellow plums. Purple Italian prune plums. Then my favorite, the freestone peaches. Pears and apples ripening into the fall.

By the end of the day, my bare arms dripped with fruit juices, gluing down cherry stems and grass to my skin. Even strands of my hair were crisp with fruit juice. Novenka and I pedaled home slowly, drenched in sweat, our bellies aching from eating too many cherries. Ma made me soak in the tub a good long while afterward.

The new land Frank had bought was across the street from Corman's. Burdock grew high and brush overtook the place that summer. But Frank was busy with the new house. First, the foundation was laid. The house was built slowly, brick by brick, by the men in my family. Frank had to wait for each week's paycheck to buy more materials. Some bricks, borrowed from a friend, he laid side by side with new ones, mixing old luck with new. He set his iron hammer down, the one he had brought from the old country, and cemented it into the basement. That hammer had been his ticket into Canada. They had let him into the country because he had a trade—carpentry. He and my brothers did all the woodwork themselves. It would take Frank over a year to build the house that way.

By the next spring, we drove out to the land some evenings and stayed all day Saturday and Sunday to help Frank with the house. We always took a carload when we went there, all the cousins and aunts and uncles joining us like we were going on a hayride instead of to work. Ma left the boarders on their own all weekend now. She was itching to settle that new land too.

I told Ma I didn't want to baby-sit anymore. I wanted to work with the men. Eddie was exploring every acre on his knees, and Pauline, in diapers, wanted to stick every stone into her mouth. Ma put Margaret in charge of them. It was her turn now. I ran out to the field to join the men, screaming all the way, "I'm free!"

Uncle Matt, Joe and Phillip were clearing two acres for an orchard far behind the house, prying out huge boulders with crowbars. They piled them up at the back border of the property, building a rock wall with them. My job was to gather all the weeds they unearthed and cart them to a compost pile beside the new garden. Up and down the rows of the garden and orchard, Frank plowed, breaking ground that had not been planted before. We followed in his trail, forever picking up boulders, rusty nails, ragweed and even old arrowheads. Huge clumps of dirt remained that we had to hack with hoes and pitchforks. By the end of the day, we were all so sore, we could barely move.

Other people pitched in to help with the work. The boys from Corman's farm. Mr. Best, a gentleman farmer with a fancy cane, our new neighbor across the highway. He gave us advice about the direction in which to plant an orchard: in rows running north to south. Phillip brought his girlfriend, Mary, and we all held our breath. But Ma liked her right away. Soon, Mary was calling her Ma and listening to everything she said. Friends always tagged along with William and his girlfriend, Audrey, too, but none of them liked to work, except Johnnie.

Johnnie came out all the time, on his bike. He'd already pedaled to Niagara Falls and back many times. He was handsome, I thought, with bright blue eyes and blond hair. He was filled out with wide shoulders and muscular arms, the opposite of my skinny younger brother. He could lift the biggest boulders from that orchard. Neither Uncle Matt nor Joe could keep up with him. He liked to tease me as I sifted out rocks on my knees about whether I'd like to baby-sit the boulder he was carrying while he took a snooze. It got to be that as soon as I saw him coming, I'd laugh, wondering what he'd be up to next.

Frank and I staked out the orchard together when the ground was churned smooth enough. I held the marker tight while Frank walked down the row with a string, lining it up square with my guidepost. He'd stand a good long while, measuring the distance between each new tree and each new row.

"I grew up planting trees in the Black Forest," he told me. "Set them in the ground just like this. Planted one for every ten we cut down."

As he dug a deep hole in a new spot, I watched him. He reminded me of Ma working the garden in Cobalt. He worked slow and steady, pitting his strength against the dirt. Whenever he set a tree into the ground, he'd pour manure all around it. He'd pat that tree down like it was a baby. Then he'd wipe the sweat from his forehead and grin at me, his face soft and shining.

"There's another one in, Frances. We'll eat good fruit from this tree in a few years."

We'd move on to the next one. Frank could work for hours and hours without a break. When he worked, he was somewhere else, same as when he fixed things. Suspended. I'm not sure he took a breath. But I whirred back and forth between Ma and him like a hummingbird. She insisted I bring Frank water and a snack. But he wouldn't stop, not even to smoke. He aimed to plant the whole row first.

We worked like farmers did, as long as we had the light. Long past dusk, we'd till the soil and carry boulders until we couldn't see anymore. As we worked that spring, the days grew longer so that by late June, we'd finish after ten o'clock. In summer, the light lingered long after sunset. It set a glow on the land, a soft red light to work by.

As the rows of trees began to stretch out in front of us, I thought how the trees seemed like soldiers lined up, tall and straight, but thin and unformed. They were like the children who had gone so young to the Civil War, marching one behind the other. I prayed that my brothers and Johnnie would not ever have to go to war. That's all anyone whispered about now that Canada would soon join the war. That summer, all the boys in our family were just the right age to be drafted.

But Mr. Best had made us see the orchard differently. He told us that if a man plants an apple tree, he will live to see its end. Apple trees can live fifty years or more, he said. Ma told Frank to plant as many apples as he could, to make sure he lived a good long while. The two of them would turn old together here, she said, and all the kids would grow into adults. I could see they planned to settle there forever. There'd be no more moving around, searching for something better.

By midsummer, Frank and I stood side by side at dusk admiring the young orchard we had planted together. The trees were taking, he said, for some had already sprouted new leaves. In each row, a different fruit grew. A row of Bartlett pears. Two rows of black cherries and sour cherries. One of apricots. Rows and rows of Macoun and McIntosh apples. Frank had left wide spaces between the rows for the trees to grow.

"Five years from now," he said, "those trees will reach out and touch one another, making a canopy between them. You kids will run beneath their blossoms, for they will have outgrown even Phillip by then. All your children will eat this fruit."

We turned around to check on everyone. Johnnie stood by the garden, his eyes on me, I thought. William teased me that all his friend did was talk about me. It was past dark by then and Ma was waving to us to come back. All day she and my brothers had pruned the old grapes and tied the vines up on a new fence, bringing them back to life. Frank and I trudged back to them, barely seeing an inch in front of our feet.

"This is the place I dreamed about before I came to Canada," he told me. "I couldn't have done it without you and your family to help me. Now we can all enjoy it. I wouldn't have believed it'd be so beautiful out here either, like a slice of heaven."

I held tight to his arm to steady myself.

"It's the farm Ma's always wanted," I said. And then in a whisper, I added, "Me too."

I could tell even in the darkness that Frank was beaming.

Ma had a campfire blazing by the oak tree, our jackets waiting and dinner heated. She had cooked extra all week. We wolfed that food down. Cabbage rolls. Sweet sausage. Pierogies fried in onions steaming hot. Always dessert. Oatmeal cookies huge as your hand. Sugared strawberries dripped over angel food cake.

We huddled with blankets over our shoulders, Poochie warming my feet. Somehow Johnnie always ended up sitting right next to me. All of us kids so glad just to sit down and sip hot tea while the men puffed on cigarettes, blowing smoke rings into the cool night air.

Someone would always begin. Perhaps Uncle Matt with a story about fishing up north. Or Joe with a spooky story from Severin. Then everyone joined in. Stories of the Black Forest, Calumet and Cobalt too. The forever long winters inside our cabin. Groundhog stew. The wolves howling in the distance. Stories told about Hamilton for the first time. Phillip telling about his job at Westinghouse where he assembled air brakes for trains. But now that war was starting, he would make torpedo engines instead. Frank spoke about how the price of food was going up and everyone was stocking up on sugar, coffee and staples, for they would ration them soon.

Then it was Poochie's turn. She was so excited on that farm, running the acres all day, chasing birds as we worked. In the light of the campfire, I joined my hands for a hoop with Poochie following me, barking and leaping through. How Ma laughed from deep in her belly, along with Aunt Tracey, the sound of it spilling out for miles around.

Then all the cousins would curl up on sleeping bags while the adults talked on and on. We could have lain there forever, listening to the stories, the voices going in and out. Our heads touching. The young ones asleep on our bellies, arms and legs in all directions. Margaret and

I whispering. Novenka giggling. Phillip's arm around Mary. Watching our breath lift up like clouds into the sky. The sky dotted with stars, the constellations so clear, we could point them out; Phillip knew all their names.

It was after midnight when we got up to go back to Hamilton. Johnnie pulled me to my feet and I leaned heavily against him on the way to the car, half asleep, wondering why we had to leave now, just now, when I was so close to having dreams touch me like angel wings. Even the farm seemed like a dream.

I didn't want to leave this land, not for a second, to go back to the grime that was Hamilton. I could hardly wait until the house was finished and we moved out here. My hands had carried the rocks and smoothed the soil and hoed around the newly planted pumpkin plants. I had set the fruit trees square with Frank so that they could bake in the southern sun and blossom next spring.

War was coming. But we would be safe here with all the growing things. This land was home.

Chapter 46
Last Visit
Fall 1938

That fall, Ma decided it was time to visit Cobalt. No one we knew lived there anymore but she said she had something to do. She packed an extra dress for her and me and dug up some peonies from a friend's yard. I scarcely slept all week long, waiting to see my old home. Frank drove us the long miles up north. It was night when we arrived. The air was so cool, our breath steamed. The mountains lined up on the horizon, like guards watching us. But most of all I remember the stars filling the sky, so bright and low down, they seemed to touch our shoulders.

The next morning, I awoke before anyone else and rushed outside to the wooden sidewalks of the town. You could barely step on them anymore. They were rotted out. I walked down the dirt road past the tenements. They were weathered gray and falling down. Most were abandoned. Broken windows stared like empty eyes. Not a single flower bloomed. It was a ghost town. Here and there, old miners stumbled along, thin and bedraggled, with full beards, heads bowed down. Their lips were flat, like they weren't used to talking anymore. They looked up at me with bloodshot eyes.

We visited our cabin far off down the road. The ever-greens had grown so tall, they made a dark blanket of shade over it. The sunlight never shone on that cabin anymore. It was empty and alone, like a lost child out in the woods. Moss crept on all sides of it. Ma guessed from the way it leaned over, it would fall to the ground within a year. Above our heads, the evergreens waved, so tall and powerful, the only living things around.

Then we headed to the cemetery. The grass was higher than our waists. Here and there, a tall tombstone stuck up. We wove our way to the back of the cemetery, following Frank, who cut a path for us with a scythe. Ma seemed to know exactly where she was going. It had been thirteen years since she last stepped foot in that cemetery, but she picked her way through weeds and burdock without halting. We spotted the lilac soaring up, its dried blossoms waving in the air.

There was no sign of Pa's tombstone.

"It's close to the trunk of that lilac." Ma pointed.

Frank swung his scythe slowly now, cutting into the weeds until we heard the scrape of metal against stone. He knelt down and yanked at the grass with his bare hands.

"Here it is. It stood up all these years. The engraving is still clear."

He made way for Ma. She glided toward the stone poking out of the ground. Thin flat slate with Pa's name on it. She stood in front of it, holding her hands to her belly, and then she drew them tightly to her heart.

Frank moved back. In the distance, we could hear his scythe swish through the tall grasses. I stepped beside Ma, my tears falling all at once, without my being ready for them. The two of us looked down. She was crying too.

"You asked me once why we left Cobalt so abruptly. I never told you why," Ma whispered in the still cemetery. "It was because of a dream."

She said she dreamed she was at a holding place. That's a room at a port or border with a roped-off area where immigrants are held when they enter or leave the country. She had gone to holding areas many times to greet relatives coming over from Croatia. Hundreds of folks swarm around in their best clothes, carrying suitcases. Everyone looks solemn at such a place, wondering if they'll be allowed to come in as they planned, worrying if their papers are in order. She roamed around such a place lost in her dream. She kept looking around, waiting for someone. For a long while, she saw no one she knew.

Then suddenly, she said, she felt someone's eyes upon her. She spun around. Across the room, Pa stood all alone with a suitcase in his hand. But he stood behind a rope so that Ma could not get near him. He looked about twenty-four years old, strong and healthy, smiling like on the day they met. The very air glowed around him.

"I'm leaving now, Frances. It's time. I can't wait any longer." He looked over his shoulder at an open doorway. Immigrants disappeared through it and never returned.

She didn't speak one word to him. It was the first dream she had of Pa where he was young and happy. In all her other dreams, he was broken and crushed. She just marveled at him now. He looked right through her, like he knew what she felt.

"I've worried about you and the kids," he said. "That's why I stayed. But they're calling me and I put it off as long as I could. I have to go. You'll be all right now. You're stronger than you know."

He tipped his fedora at her and walked right through that doorway. He had a look on his face like he was expecting a miracle. He was all lit up, she said. I suppose angels look just like that.

"The very next morning when I awoke, I felt ready to move on," Ma remembered. "I opened the windows wide. I didn't know it would upset you so. You screamed and cried yourself to sleep that day."

I spoke up then, telling the secret I'd held in the shadows.

"Pa was here with us in Cobalt. He was with me from the first, when I was just born. I knew he left that day too. But I didn't know why."

Ma gasped. Her eyes grew very dark and she searched my face as if she were trying to look through me. "You knew your pa was with us? How could you know such a thing?"

"He spoke to me just before I was born. He told me to come to you. That you needed someone to pull you back from your sadness. And then he stayed. I felt it in the air all around me."

Ma's hand touched my shoulder and I felt it tremble.

"Sometimes, in that cabin, I felt him just as if he never left. I thought I was the only one who knew," she said.

She hugged me tight and then slowly released me. We stared at each other a long while, almost as if we had never seen each other before, although we had lived side by side all these years.

I felt something drop down out of me then. Something I had held on to for so long. Pa had left me that morning, without saying good-bye, I thought. Up until that day, I had tiptoed through Cobalt like I was in heaven with him. But he had said good-bye to my mother. I could have let him go, if only I had known.

I looked around me then and saw the whole cemetery cleared now, hundreds of tombstones sticking up everywhere in the spiky weeds. The dead outnumbered the living in this ghost town. Beside me, Ma had her hands folded and her eyes shut. I left her on her own to say her prayers.

As I wandered around, one by one, the angels popped up on the tombstones, almost as if they'd stopped down in flight right in front of me. Their bodies were scarred by snow and wind but their stone eyes plainly stared at me. So many of them, with me walking in their midst. They were just as my brother had described them. There was such a silence around them, a peace, from another world. I stood as still as them and listened.

And what I heard was that Pa was not there in that ground anymore. He had moved on, like us. He lived in May blossoms, the summer wind blowing across Aunt

Annie's wheat field, and the cold waves tossing on Lake Ontario's blue face.

The spirits didn't live in Cobalt anymore. Nobody paid attention to them. No one looked up to the sky and prayed. The light had died in folks there.

And then I knew. The spirits are everywhere. All you have to do is call for them.

There was a place I could do that now. Plant my feet down and lift my voice up to be heard. A place that was soon to be home. Stoney Creek. Frank said we'd harvest the grapes after the first hard frost and bake our pumpkins into pie. We had invited Johnnie over for Thanksgiving. He'd been drafted into the navy and would leave for the East Coast at the end of October. But he'd asked me to cycle to Niagara Falls with him before he left. Thirty-eight miles and back again in one day with a picnic lunch in our bike baskets. I'd been waiting for the right moment to ask Ma to go. I knew I could ask her now, on the way home.

I rushed back to Ma's side and said a last prayer to Pa, the tears streaming now, the tears I'd squeezed inside since Schumacher. When I was finished, I looked at Pa's tombstone. I couldn't help smiling through my tears. I was all lit up inside, like one of the angels. I wanted Pa to see me like this. Everything was ahead of me now. Even the spirits. I could have twirled right then and there as I used to when I was a child in Cobalt. But I kept still and waited for Ma.

I watched her bow her head down a good long time.

She had left her black dress behind, but she didn't ever want to forget Pa. She wanted his blessing to go ahead. Ma must have received an answer from Pa, for she busied herself around the stone, yanking out more weeds. Frank came over then, his hands moving in the dirt beside hers. He shoveled a hole and sank the peonies in the ground, their glossy green leaves resting against the stone.

"It's a pretty spot," Frank admired. "Phillip has a fine resting place."

He reached down for Ma's arm to lift her up. They looked into each other's eyes. It was only then, standing side by side, that I noticed they both had blue eyes. Ma's eyes were china blue. Frank's were a see-through blue, almost green. They sighed, like something was over. I stepped on the other side of my mother, squeezing her arm, and she squeezed me back. We both led her away. We walked smoothly together, our feet in step, finding our way back on the perfect path Frank had cut.

We stepped out into a clear blue Cobalt day.

Epilogue:
Keeper of the Stories

We had two weddings in August 1940. Phillip married Mary, and the next day, my mother married Frank. My brother and his new wife moved into our old house on Birmingham Street. The rest of us moved out to the farm in Stoney Creek.

Frank sprinkled salt over the doorstep of our new brick house like it was a bride too. Salt is life, he told us; we can't live without it. He bought Bessie, a milk cow, and a flock of bantam chickens that always skittered about. Ma planted peonies in front, a splash of maroon beside the bleeding heart bush. From our kitchen window, we can breathe in the smell of lilacs when they bloom on the south side. A memory of sweetness and sadness mixed together from long ago.

Phillip was drafted into the army by 1941. He was gone a whole long year to Labrador, guarding the coast of Canada. When he returned in 1942 on a week's furlough, we all had to have our photograph taken. Ma insisted. We had something to celebrate. My niece Myrna, Phillip's daughter, was a year old by then, and she sat on my mother's lap, the first grandchild, while we gathered around in our Sunday best, our faces brightly lit by the child's laughter.

There were so many jobs available once the boys were drafted into the army. The factories nearly closed down without them. So all the women in Hamilton went out to work in the factories to help the war effort. I crafted bullets at Westinghouse to ship to the soldiers in Europe. Every week, I mailed letters to the front, writing to boys I had never met, telling them to come home safe. I wrote about the first peaches ripening on our trees, Ma's sour cherry pie, and the new church, library and school being built across the street. Canada was a growing place just waiting for their return.

By then, William was engaged to his childhood sweetheart, Audrey, and Helen was married to Stan. Even Novenka had a wedding date set. They all teased me and said I would be next. I was in love with Poochie, the lake, the flat farmland and literature, I told them. I wouldn't confess that I could hardly wait to see Johnnie when he came home on weekend leave. He was so handsome in his uniform and gentle too, like I imagined my own pa had been. Everyone said he would ask me to marry him soon.

I never want to leave the fruit belt. Fertile land that runs east to west like the sun, holding my dreams. I plan to spend the rest of my life here and grow old with the orchard. Whoever I marry must understand that. How I lived all that time in cold faraway places, only to find a real home now.

One afternoon, I walked through the orchard in the bright light of a spring day. Blossom Sunday. So cool, I had to wear a jacket. Up and down the rows, the fruit trees, loaded with blossoms, lifted their arms one by one. Like promises of fruit to come. Pink apple flowers. Dark red blossoms of the black cherry tree. White pear clusters. They waved in the air, their colors crisp against the bare brown earth. The air heated up with their perfume. It blew sweet and fresh for miles around. Everything was growing around me.

Then I felt it. The wind picking up, rustling the blossoms.

I recognized it now. How it drops down from unseen places, places where it might have touched God, and floats away again to infinity. It passed right through me with a shiver. The spirits were flying by. Glowing through the air, making it bright with light. I have stood here beneath these trees and on that flat land and called for them to come. My body so still, listening for an answer.

I have to be near growing things. I have to fill myself with the stories like bits of silver gleaming in the dark. I have had to sigh my sorrows out too and let just the light back in.

That spring, I felt I had passed through something, leaving my old self behind. It was as if I had finally walked through a door that had always been locked before. One day, I just touched my fingers to the handle and found it turned so easily in my grasp. I knew everything was possible then.

> *Our birth is but a sleep and a forgetting:*
> *The Soul that rises with us, our life's Star,*
> *Hath had elsewhere its setting,*
> *And cometh from afar:*
> *Not in entire forgetfulness,*
> *And not in utter nakedness,*
> *But trailing clouds of glory do we come*
> *From God, who is our home.*

> Wordsworth,
> from *Intimations*
> *of Immortality*